Dark Memories

by

Linda Hope Lee

This is a work of fiction. Names, characters, places, and incidents are either the product of the author's imagination or are used fictitiously, and any resemblance to actual persons living or dead, business establishments, events, or locales, is entirely coincidental.

Dark Memories

COPYRIGHT © 2016 by Linda Hope Lee

Cover Art by *Kristian Norris*

The Wild Rose Press, Inc.
PO Box 708
Adams Basin, NY 14410-0708
Visit us at www.thewildrosepress.com

Publishing History
First Crimson Rose Edition, 2016
Print ISBN 978-1-5092-0645-2
Digital ISBN 978-1-5092-0646-9

Published in the United States of America

She went through the house,
checking the locks on the doors and windows, and drawing the curtains. In the kitchen, as she reached over the sink to close the blinds, she saw movement outside. Was someone in her yard?

Her heart thumping, Deborah stared out into the dark night, studying the yard. Nothing. All was still. Perhaps she had seen only her own reflection in the window.

Her feeling of unease remained, though, and after turning off the overhead lights, plunging the kitchen into darkness, she crept back to the sink and peered between the blinds' slats. Her gaze swept the yard, settling on the hedge between her property and the Healys' housing development. A shadow shifted. Was someone hiding behind the hedge?

Sure enough, in the next moment a figure slunk from the bushes into the open. He—or she—wore black clothing, gloves, and a knit ski mask with only slits for eyes, nose, and mouth. The person turned toward the kitchen window.

Deborah shuddered and ducked out of sight. Her heart hammered and her throat dried. She let a few seconds elapse and then eased upright. She inched to the window and again peeked through the blinds' slats.

The person was still in the yard. He pranced around, waving his arms and kicking his feet through the pile of leaves she raked earlier that week. Oh, oh, now he aimed toward the back door. Footsteps thudded up the steps and across the porch. The doorknob rattled and shook.

Praise for Linda Hope Lee

"A modern western, packed with secrets, intrigue and old-fashioned romance. [*FINDING SARA*] is a romance that won't be forgotten."

~Joanne Hall, Writers and Readers
of Distinctive Fiction

~*~

"Lee takes a cowboy and an heiress and combines them into a refreshingly sweet tale. Readers can easily relate to the main characters as Sara searches for herself while Jackson overcomes a devastating loss."

~Karen Sweeny-Justice, Romantic Times (4 Stars)

~*~

"[LOVING ROSE] is a sweet, heartwarming read that will tug at your heartstrings."

~Melissa, Sizzlinghotbookreviews.net (4 Hearts)

~*~

"What a beautiful story! [*LOVING ROSE*] is full of characters who face real-life situations."

~Nikki, sirenbookreviews.blogspot.com
(4.5 Siren Stones)

Dedication

To Billy

Chapter One

On a warm day in September, Deborah Kent drove her silver SUV along the winding country road connecting Castletown to Fairfield, Vermont. As she'd hoped, the Castletown flea market was an excellent place to find furniture for the bed-and-breakfast she planned to open in January. The oak rocking chair and matching end tables she purchased were secured in the rear of the vehicle.

Instead of traveling Highway 89, she chose a side road where she could enjoy the beauty of the autumn countryside. The scenery was spectacular. Maple and aspen trees blazed with red, orange, and yellow leaves, while in the distance, purple hills rose into a cobalt blue sky dotted with puffy white clouds.

Then, as she slowed to navigate a curve, the SUV's engine sputtered and lost power. Deborah stepped on the accelerator, but the car continued to inch along. She barely made it to the side of the road before the vehicle lurched to a stop.

Stunned, Deborah sat there staring at the swirls of dust rising from underneath the tires. Why would the car quit so suddenly? She switched the ignition off and then on again. The engine ground but would not catch. She tried several times with the same result.

An icy chill washed over her. Could this problem be related to the note she'd found stuck in her screen door last week? Closing her eyes, she pictured the note's bold printing:

GET OUT OF TOWN OR YOU'LL END UP LIKE CARLA CASSIDY.

Deborah did not want to share Carla Cassidy's fate. The young woman's tragic death was the reason Deborah left Fairfield four years ago. Now she was back, intending to once again make the small town her home.

The cruel note told her someone didn't want her to return.

Several people who might have written the note had come to mind. After a week passed with no further warnings, Deborah was ready to dismiss the threat as a prank.

Now she was having car trouble. Coincidence? Or connected to the note?

Whatever, she must deal with her immediate problem, and soon. She looked around. Not a car in sight. No way did she want to linger on this isolated road.

Car mechanics were a foreign language to her, so no use looking under the hood. She'd have to call for help. Reaching into her purse lying on the passenger's seat, she pulled out her cell phone, switched it on, and spotted a red X, indicating no phone service. Disappointing, but no real surprise, considering the hills and thick woods surrounding this rural area.

Peering through the windshield, she glimpsed the silver silo and red barn of a farm about a mile away. Someone there would have a phone she could use. She pulled her keys from the ignition, grabbed her purse, and stepped from the SUV. An ominous stillness greeted her. Despite the sunshine, gooseflesh speckled her skin, making her shiver and rub her arms.

She'd no more than locked the door and started off when the clatter of a horse's hooves broke the silence. Turning, she spotted a sleek, black horse, with the rider sitting tall, trotting along the road. Maybe he could help.

When they reached her side, the rider reined his mount to a halt.

The man looked to be in his thirties, with deep-set dark eyes and thick, black hair. He wore a denim shirt, jeans, and brown leather boots.

"Car trouble?" He nodded in the direction of her SUV.

She pursed her lips and nodded. "It suddenly quit. I intended to call for help, but my cell phone won't work."

"Reception here is a problem. I'll take a look at your car. I'm no mechanic, but if it's something simple, I might be able to fix it."

His deep voice rang with friendliness, and if Deborah's instincts were on target, his gaze held more than a hint of male interest. Despite her annoyance with the car breakdown, she experienced a tingle of excitement. "I'd appreciate that, if you're sure it's no trouble."

He lifted a shoulder. "Not at all. Black Magic and I are just out for an afternoon ride with no particular destination."

"All right." Relieved to find help so soon, Deborah offered him a smile.

The man dismounted his horse. Reins in hand, he fell into step beside her as they headed toward her car.

Taller than she, he was about six feet, she judged, and in his mid-thirties.

He slanted her a glance. "Do you live around here?"

"In Fairfield."

"I get the feeling you're new in the area. Am I right?"

"Sort of. I used to live in Fairfield a few years ago." Unwilling to share details of her absence from Fairfield with a stranger, Deborah kept her reply brief. Before either of them could say more, they reached her car.

"What happened when your car quit running?" he asked as he tied the reins to the guardrail.

While she explained the car's behavior, Deborah unlocked the driver's side door and then handed him the keys.

He climbed in and settled behind the wheel, his broad shoulders filling the seat. When he twisted the key in the ignition, the engine made only a dull, rasping noise. He looked up with a frown.

She nodded. "That's exactly what happened when I tried to restart it."

"I'll check under the hood." He reached below the dashboard to pull the hood release.

Waiting for him to complete his inspection, Deborah paced, glancing at him now and then when he mumbled something under his breath. Dare she hope he could take care of the problem and she could soon be on her way?

After a few minutes, he straightened and shook his head. "Sorry, I don't see anything I can fix. Could be a bad fuel pump. For that, you'll need professional help."

Deborah stuffed down her disappointment and considered her next option. "Thanks for trying. I'll have the car towed to a garage in Fairfield. I was on my way to the farm down the road, to use the phone." She pointed toward the silver silo.

Grinning, he pulled a handkerchief from his back jeans pocket and wiped his hands. "That's my place. I'll phone for a tow truck and then drive you to home."

Deborah stiffened. "I don't want to put you out. I can hitch a ride with the tow truck."

"I don't mind."

He offered her a persuasive smile. Still, Deborah hesitated to accept his invitation. He appeared sincere, but he was a stranger. And, there was that note…

The man's gaze shifted to her vehicle. "Don't worry about leaving your car and that furniture here. Just be sure to lock up."

"I'm not worried about that."

Understanding glimmered in his dark eyes. "Okay, I get it. You're afraid to go off with a stranger, right? Don't blame you. Can't be too careful these days. But, let me introduce myself, and then we won't be strangers anymore. I'm Milo Jordan." He extended his hand.

Milo Jordan. The strong, masculine name suited him. "I'm Deborah," she offered, as she shook his hand.

"Pleased to meet you. So, how about it?" He nodded toward his farm. "You letting me do my good deed for the day?"

Still, she hesitated. The warning note, the car breaking down, the sudden appearance of a handsome man to help her. Coincidence? Or part of a plan engineered by whoever wanted to torment her?

Yet, Milo's open and friendly face made her doubt

he could be involved in any plot. Maybe the note and the car breakdown were connected, but surely, this man had nothing to do with either. "I wouldn't want to keep you from your good deeds," she said in a teasing tone.

"All ri-i-ght. Do you want to ride Black Magic?" He gestured to his horse. "Or would you rather walk?"

Deborah glanced at the horse. "I don't mind walking."

"Me, neither."

She locked her car, and he untied Black Magic, and then they started off down the road in the direction of his farm.

"You said you used to live in Fairfield." Milo matched her steps as they walked along. "Are you back for good now?"

"I hope so. I'm turning an old house into a bed-and-breakfast."

"Sounds like a lot of work."

"It is, but the remodeling is fun, too."

"Fun." He tossed back his head and laughed. "That's what I told myself when I was remodeling my house. When I bought the place a few years ago, I knew it needed a lot of work. But I had the time, and so I decided to do most of it myself."

They talked some more about house renovating, and soon turned onto a narrow lane that led through a grove of maple trees to Milo's farm.

When she reached the house, Deborah stopped and gazed at the two-story home. The white clapboard siding and shake roof sparkled in the sunlight. On the porch, pots of red geraniums, white wicker furniture, and a swing hanging from the ceiling provided homey touches. She turned to Milo. "This is charming. You did a superb job with your remodeling."

He met her gaze with a grin. "Thanks. I'm happy with the result—and glad it's done."

Milo led Deborah around the house to the back yard where flowers spilled from a wire-fenced garden and several ducks squawked a greeting from a pond rimmed with white-painted stones. A peaked-roof stable stood nearby, and next to that, a pen filled with bales of hay.

He pointed to the house's back door. "Go on in while I take care of Black Magic. My housekeeper is most likely in the kitchen. Her name is Katie, and she'll keep you company until I come in."

"All right. But where will I find a phone?"

"No need for you to call. I'll phone Johnson's Auto Repair from the stable. Johnny's a friend of mine."

"But you've already done so much—"

"Glad to help." He waved a hand. "I'll join you in a few minutes."

Deborah went inside and down a short hallway to the kitchen where a gray-haired woman wearing jeans and a print blouse stood at the sink. The paring knife in her hand flew as she peeled potatoes and dropped them into a pot of water. The aroma of something that smelled like cake baking in the oven filled the air. She called out, "Hello. You must be Katie."

Paring knife suspended, Katie turned and gave a raised-eyebrow look. "I am. And who are you?"

Deborah introduced herself, adding, "I had car trouble, and Milo's calling a tow truck."

"That's Milo." Katie rolled her eyes. "He loves to help people, but he likes to take charge, too."

Deborah laughed, glad her instincts had been right

about Milo. "So I'm finding out."

"Have a seat." Katie nodded at a round wooden table and chairs occupying a sunlit corner.

Deborah pulled out a chair and sat, and Katie returned to peeling her potatoes. She was friendly and talkative, and they chatted until Milo came in.

"I called Johnny," he told Deborah, "and he's sending a tow truck to pick up your car. We don't need to be there. After I take you home, I'll drop off your keys. Then you can give them a call and see what they found out."

Hardly pausing for breath, he rubbed his hands together and added, "Now, how about a cup of coffee and some of Kate's cranberry bread? I can smell it baking. Or are you in a rush to get home?"

Deborah considered his invitation. Earlier, she was eager to get home, but now, spending more time in Milo Jordan's company, here in his cozy farmhouse, tempted her. "No, I'm not in any hurry."

Kate put down her paring knife and wiped her hands on a dishtowel. "Good timing, Milo. The bread's just done. Go sit in the front room, you two, and I'll bring it in with some coffee."

In the front room, Milo waved Deborah toward several leather chairs and a sofa grouped around a beech wood coffee table. Deborah sank into one of the chairs and gazed around. Low book shelves and framed western prints filled one wall, while across the room a picture window looked out on a grassy yard.

Katie bustled in carrying a tray. She handed them each a plate with a piece of bread and a mug of coffee and then returned to the kitchen.

Deborah sampled the bread. Still warm, full of

cranberries and nuts and with a spicy aroma, it melted in her mouth. "Mmm, this hits the spot."

"Katie's the best." Milo picked up his mug and took a sip. "I'm lucky to have her."

"What kind of farming do you do?"

"No farming to speak of. I raise horses. For riding, not racing."

"Really? How'd you get into the business?"

"My grandfather raised horses. I visited him a lot when I was a kid and grew to share his interest. After I got out of the army, I came back to Fairfield and bought this farm." He made a sweeping gesture toward the picture window.

As Deborah listened to Milo talk about his farm and horses, she leaned back and relaxed against the cool leather. She even allowed herself to daydream a little. He seemed such a congenial person, not to say handsome and appealing. Perhaps they could forge a friendship. She doubted there was a Mrs. Jordan. If a wife existed, surely he would have mentioned her by now.

Deborah's spirits lifted, and the car breakdown took on a fortuitous, rather than a negative, aspect.

After a while, Milo paused to level his dark-eyed gaze on Deborah. "I've been going on about myself and haven't learned much about you. Only that you lived here before and are fixing up a bed-and-breakfast. Did you recently buy the house?"

Deborah studied her coffee cup as she considered what to tell him. She must be careful to not say too much. She feared he wouldn't be interested in her if he knew about Carla and the accident. "The woman who owned the house was my guardian," she said. "She passed away a few months ago and left me the house in her will."

"I see." He waited, eyebrows raised.

The gesture meant he obviously expected more. But as far as Deborah was concerned, she had already revealed enough. Of course, if they continued their association, he would eventually learn more. But not now. Not when they'd just met. She set her mug and empty plate on the coffee table. "This has been really pleasant, but I should be going."

"Really? Well, okay. If you must." Disappointment shadowed his eyes.

Oh, oh, maybe she was being too sensitive, too cautious.

But then he smiled again. "Come out some other time. We'll go riding."

"I'd like that."

Their gazes met and they exchanged smiles. Warmth flowed through Deborah, renewing the hope that they might establish a friendship yet.

Milo put his plate and cup on the coffee table and stood. "Wait here while I get my car keys, and then we'll be on our way."

When she was alone, Deborah walked to the picture window and gazed out. Several maple trees shaded an expanse of grass. Lawn chairs, a picnic table, and a portable barbecue were grouped together, offering a place to relax and enjoy an outdoor meal.

She turned back to the room, and her gaze fell on the bookshelves. Curious to know Milo's taste in reading, she approached the nearest section. Tipping back her head, she studied the titles. His taste ran from western and mystery novels to history and, not surprisingly, the care and training of horses.

On the shelf above, a gold-framed photo caught her eye. At first, she focused on the pretty frame, with its delicate, embossed flowers. Then she moved her gaze to the picture, a portrait of a teenage girl. Dark, curly hair framed an oval face with large brown eyes and a wide, expressive mouth. Recognition clanged like a bell in Deborah's mind, and she gasped.

Carla Cassidy.

But no, the girl couldn't be Carla.

She was mistaken. She *had* to be mistaken.

With shaking hands, Deborah picked up the picture and gave it closer scrutiny.

No doubt about it, the teen was Carla Cassidy. But why was her picture on Milo's bookshelf? Were they related? They could be. They had the same thick, black hair, the same brown eyes.

Deborah had met Carla's mother and stepfather and heard Carla had an older brother. But at the time of the accident, he'd been overseas in the army. For some reason—illness, maybe—he did not come home for the funeral.

Milo said he'd been in the army. He must be the older brother.

Nausea churned in Deborah's stomach and the room closed in. She must get out of there. *Now.*

"Okay, I'm ready to go." Milo's cheerful voice rang out from the doorway.

Deborah froze, gripping the picture so hard the embossed flowers on the frame dug into her fingers.

"What's the matter?" Milo crossed the room to her side. "You look as though you'd seen a ghost."

When she didn't reply, she watched his gaze leave

her face and travel to the picture. She braced herself for what he might say next.

His eyes clouded and his shoulders sagged. "That's my sister, Carla. She died in an accident while she was attending Wainwright Academy. That's an exclusive girls' school nearby. Maybe you've heard of it."

"Yes," she whispered. "I have…heard of it."

"She and her classmates were on a fieldtrip to Rainbow Falls," Milo went on. "Carla fell from a cliff and landed at the bottom of the falls…" He looked away to gaze out the window.

A black cloud of despair settled over Deborah. No use hiding the truth any longer. She swallowed hard. "I k-know…about the accident."

"You know?"

Milo's narrowed eyes pinned her like an insect trapped by a collector's pin. Trembling, she met his gaze.

Finally, he spoke. "Okay, I just figured it out. You're Deborah Kent. And you know about Carla's death because you're the teacher who is responsible."

Chapter Two

Milo folded his arms and stared at the young woman he'd rescued and brought to his home. He hoped Deborah would deny the charge. She didn't. Instead, she remained silent, her eyes downcast.

Often, he dreamed of confronting the woman responsible for Carla's tragic accident. He wanted to see what kind of woman she was. He wanted to vent his anger and frustration.

Now she was in his presence, and he only wanted her out of his sight. He pried the picture from her hands and set it back on the shelf. The smiling face of his dead sister brought tightness to his chest. "I'll take you home now," he said through clenched teeth.

Expecting her to follow, he marched from the room to the front door, and then down the steps to his car parked in the driveway. As he opened the passenger's door, he realized she was not behind him, as he'd thought. He turned back to the house.

She stood at the bottom of the steps, clutching the railing. "You don't have to take me home," she said in a monotone. "I can call a taxi."

Her eyes were as bleak as a cold winter's day. Her offer tempted him. But when he met her on the road, he said he would help her. His sense of responsibility prompted him to follow through. "I said I'd take you home, and I will," he said. "But let's get a move on."

Once they were on their way, Milo shook his head in disbelief at the day's events. He began the afternoon in high spirits with a leisurely ride on Black Magic along the back road to Castletown. Then he encountered an attractive woman who needed help. She was about five-feet-two, and he liked petite women. Her shoulder-length blonde hair was fine and silky-looking, the kind he'd like to run his fingers through. Her facial features were delicate—pert nose, sculpted lips, and softly rounded chin. He was pleased to help her with her car trouble. They spent a pleasant time at his house, getting to know each other.

And then to learn she was Deborah Kent, the teacher involved in Carla's death. *Unbelievable.* Milo gripped the steering wheel.

Now, he wished he'd never taken the country road or spoken to the stranded woman. He glanced at her. With her head bowed and her arms folded across her chest, she appeared utterly miserable. *Too bad.* He refused to feel sorry for her. "As you must be aware, finding out who you are was a great shock."

She looked up. "I was shocked to learn who you are, too. Your last name is different from Carla's."

Milo braked for a stop sign, checked for traffic, and then stepped on the gas again. "She took our stepfather Ed Cassidy's name when he adopted her."

"You weren't around when she had her accident, were you?"

"I was in the army, stationed in Germany. I'd just had an emergency appendectomy. Complications kept me in the hospital for a couple of months. I couldn't be here to attend the funeral or the inquest, or to comfort my mother and stepfather." He'd forever regret not being able to say good-bye to his sister.

"When the inquest was over and I lost my job at Wainwright, I left town immediately," Deborah said. "That's why we never met."

"That's the way it must have happened."

"Are your mother and stepfather still living in Burlington?"

Another painful memory surfaced, and Milo tensed. "No. A couple years after Carla's death, they went on a cruise to Hawaii. They took a helicopter tour of one of the volcanoes. On the way back to the ship, the 'copter crashed." His voice dropped a notch. "There were no survivors."

She gasped and pressed a hand to her chest. "I didn't know. I'm so sorry."

Milo clamped his jaw shut. He didn't want her sympathy. He didn't want anything from this woman— except to be rid of her.

The home Deborah inherited turned out to be an old Victorian, sitting like a proud queen at the end of a cul-de-sac. Several acres of land surrounded the house, setting it well apart from neighbors. Milo parked at the curb and leaned forward to gaze out the windshield at the house. Remodeling his house had taught him a bit about architecture. This home had steeply-pitched, cross-gabled roofs, and a porch that wrapped around the sides. A turret and a widow's walk added interest to the top floor. Forgetting his anger for a moment, he commented, "Quite a place."

"It is." Deborah peered at the house from her window. "But the house needs work. I have to do a lot of painting, inside and out, as well as make other repairs."

"You said it was willed to you."

"Yes, by Rose Dobson. She became my guardian after my parents died."

So Deborah had lost both her parents, too. Sympathy nudged him, but he steeled himself against it. He didn't want to feel anything positive toward this woman. However, he was curious. "Was Rose a relative?"

"No, she was my mother's best friend. She married a man named Hank, but they had no children. After a few years, Hank disappeared and never returned."

"What about your parents?"

"They passed away when I was in high school. They were in their forties when I was born. Dad died first of a heart attack, and then Mom got cancer. When Mom passed away, Rose finished raising me. Like I said before, she died a few months ago and willed me the house. She took in boarders, so it's already set up for guests."

"Perfect location, too." He made a sweeping gesture. "The dead-end road will give your guests peace and privacy."

"I suppose you think I have no right to come back here and live."

Her angry tone tempted him to say yes, but honesty won out. "I can't make that judgment."

She reached for the door handle. "I'd better go now. Despite everything, I do appreciate all your help today."

Milo pulled the keys from the ignition and dropped them into his jacket pocket. "I'll walk you to the door."

Deborah frowned. "You don't have to. You've done enough, considering…"

He raised one eyebrow. "Considering I now know who you are? Maybe. But I won't have fulfilled my obligation to see you home until you're safely inside."

She made no further argument, and he followed her up the stone walk, past two huge maple trees and several planters filled with geraniums. They climbed the stairs to a porch furnished with white wicker and a wooden glider.

Deborah pulled a ring of keys from her shoulder purse. Opening the screen door made a slip of paper flutter to the porch. She gasped and pressed her hand over her mouth.

Milo stared at the paper lying on the porch. What could be threatening about a piece of paper? He noticed she seemed frozen, so he leaned over and retrieved it. The fold fell open in his palm, revealing a printed message:

GET OUT OF TOWN BEFORE YOU END UP LIKE CARLA.

The full meaning of the words had barely registered in his mind when Deborah snatched the paper from his hand.

She looked at the message, and her fingers trembled. "Oh, no! Not again!" she said in a choked voice.

He stepped closer and placed his hand on her shoulder. A whiff of her spicy perfume drifted past his nose. "Hey, take it easy." Seeing the fear in her eyes shocked him. "Deborah…" he began.

"I'm o-okay," she said, pulling away. Still clutching the note, she stabbed her key at the lock, but her shaking hand missed the mark.

"Give me the keys." Milo held out his hand.

Deborah hesitated for a moment longer but then placed the keys in his palm.

He unlocked the door and motioned her inside. Without waiting to be invited, he followed. The faint odor of fresh paint drifted from the back of the house.

"You don't have to stay," she said, stopping in the entryway. "I'm fine now. Really."

"I don't think so. Take a look." Grasping her shoulders, he turned her toward an oval mirror hanging above a small table.

Deborah peered at her image and pressed a hand to her pale cheek. "Oh, my."

"See what I mean? Where's the nearest place you can sit?"

"In there." She gestured to a double doorway a few steps ahead on the left.

Holding her by the hand, he led them into a living room, or parlor, as it would have been called in the old days. He looked around to get his bearings and then guided her across a threadbare rug to a worn sofa. "Sit, and I'll get you a glass of water."

Still clutching the note, Deborah sank onto the sofa.

Milo went down a dark, narrow hallway leading to the back of the house. He found the kitchen and soon returned with a glass of water. Handing it to her, he stood over her while she drank. Sunlight from the window turned her flaxen hair to silver. Her hands, one holding the glass, the other still clutching the note, had slender, tapered fingers. His chest tightened. He took a deep breath and forced his mind back to the note. "I don't blame you for being shook up," he said. "I would be, too, if I received a death threat."

She set the glass on a scarred wooden coffee table and looked up with wide eyes. "Do you really think it's a death threat?"

He shrugged. "Carla died, didn't she? And the note says that if you don't leave town, you'll end up like her."

Fine lines appeared on Deborah's smooth brow. "I know, but…" She looked down at the note in her hand.

"It's not the first note you've received, either. I heard you say 'Not again' when we were on the porch."

She sighed and pushed a lock of hair behind her ear. "No, it's not."

"Tell me about the others."

"These notes are none of your concern."

Milo folded his arms. "They're about Carla, and so they are my concern."

"Okay, I've received one other note. About a week ago, stuck in the door, same as this one."

"I want to see it."

Deborah bit her lip and looked away. Long seconds passed before she finally leaned over to an end table and opened the drawer. She rummaged around, pulled out a slip of paper, and held it out. "Here."

He raised both hands and took a step back. "I don't want to touch it. Put both of the notes on the coffee table."

"Your fingerprints are already on the new one."

"But not on this one. We need to keep it as clean as possible. The police may be able to get the person's prints."

She straightened and glared. "Who says I'm telling them?"

"Just put down the notes." He pointed to the coffee

table. "We'll discuss that later."

Deborah laid both notes on the table.

Milo sat beside her, leaned forward, and studied the messages. Both were written in block letters with a pen. The letters were perfectly formed, all the same size and in a straight line. "I'd say those letters were made with a stencil."

Deborah nodded. "I think you're right."

He sat back and looked at her. "Do you have any idea who wrote these?"

"Someone who was upset and angry with me when Carla died, I suppose. That could be any number of people."

"That was four years ago. Why is your being back in town now a threat?"

"I don't know. Please, leave it alone."

Something inside Milo snapped. He grasped her shoulders and turned her to face him. "No, I won't leave it alone. This is serious. You need to contact the police."

Deborah bit her lip. "I don't want to do that."

"I don't care. If you don't, then I will." He reached for his cell phone attached to his belt.

She placed a hand on his forearm. "No, don't call them. I will. But not now. I need a little time."

"How much time?"

"Tomorrow. I'll do it tomorrow. First thing."

Milo narrowed his eyes, not knowing whether or not to believe her. Unless he wanted to take matters into his own hands, though, he had to. "Okay," he growled. "I'm counting on you to keep your word."

"I will, I will."

Milo looked at the notes again. Even though he'd

studied the police report and spoken to those involved, he'd never been completely satisfied. The suspicion that there was more to his sister's death than was contained in any of the documentation nagged him. The notes Deborah had received confirmed his suspicions.

An idea popped into his mind, and his pulse raced. The plan involved more contact with Deborah, something he didn't really want, but if that would finally put the matter of his sister's death to rest, he'd do it. "Tell me what happened that day at Rainbow Falls."

Wide-eyed, she stiffened her shoulders and drew away. "What? Why? There are reports you can read."

"I've read them and I'm not satisfied. Something is missing. If I hear your version, I might put all the pieces together."

She fisted her hands. "I have suffered more than you could ever know because of that accident. I lost the job I loved, my home—"

"And yet, you came back."

"I told you, I returned because Rose left me the house."

"You could've sold it." He leaned back against the sofa. "No, I think there's another reason you're back in town."

"No, no." She shook her head. "And, believe me, if I'd known who you were when we first met, I never, never would've gone home with you."

"And you'd still be sitting there on the road." He gave a short, cynical laugh.

"Someone else would have eventually come along. Our meeting today was a mistake. A huge mistake."

"I don't think so. We met so that you can tell me

what happened that day."

"That's absurd."

He clenched his hands. "You owe it to me."

"You might think so, but I disagree. And, even if I wanted to tell you about that day, I couldn't right now. My head is spinning." She rubbed her forehead. "Please, I need you to leave."

Milo opened his mouth to argue but then clamped his jaw shut. He'd pushed her far enough—for now. "All right, I'll leave. But you will tell the police about these notes." He pointed to the two slips of paper on the coffee table.

"Yes," she said, her voice weary, "I will do that. Tomorrow."

"I'll call you tomorrow to make sure you did." He pulled his wallet from his back pocket, took out a business card, and laid it on the table. "Give me your phone numbers and your car keys. I'll drop them off at Johnson's on my way home."

Deborah reached into her purse and took out her business card and her keys. She dropped them into his outstretched palm.

He tucked the card into his wallet and slipped the keys into his jacket pocket. "I'll see myself out." He couldn't resist adding, "Keep this in mind, Deborah. Sooner or later, you will tell me what happened at Rainbow Falls."

Chapter Three

Deborah held her breath until she heard the front door close, and then she exhaled a long whoosh and leaned back against the sofa cushions. Since learning Milo was Carla's brother, she'd wanted only to escape his presence. She still could hardly believe she'd had the misfortune to meet him today.

Not only that, but also he wanted her to tell him about the accident.

Never.

Yet, she understood why he wanted to know everything he could about that fateful day. Carla was his sister and judging by the pain in his dark eyes when he spoke of her, he'd loved her very much.

He had questions about Carla's accident. Actually, so did Deborah. Something strange happened that day at Rainbow Falls. Something she could neither explain nor forget. She even had nightmares about the occurrence.

She didn't want to confide in Milo. Not him, of all people. He was already biased against her as the person responsible for his sister's death. Deborah's gaze fell on the notes lying on the coffee table. Their hateful message set her stomach churning. How dare someone threaten her!

She wished Milo had not been present at the discovery of the second note. He was right, though; the letters did look stenciled. He also had a point about the police needing to know about them. She would keep her promise and pay a visit to the police station tomorrow morning.

Rummaging in the end table's drawer, she found a legal-size envelope. Holding it open next to the notes, she carefully edged them inside without leaving more of her fingerprints. She doubted the writer would be stupid enough to leave his or her fingerprints on the papers, but you never knew.

Deborah had just finished dinner when a mechanic from Johnson's Auto Repair phoned.

"Your SUV had a bad fuel pump," he told her. "Luckily, we have one in stock that will fit. I'll have it fixed and delivered to you sometime tomorrow morning."

"That would be great," she said, relieved the problem was not more serious. "Did the pump wear out? The car is only four years old."

"The vacuum hose had a hole in it. Can't say for sure how it got there. Looks like something ate through the rubber. Acid, maybe."

Acid? Deborah tightened her grip on the phone. "Is there any acid in the engine area that could have dripped onto it?"

"Didn't find any. But we'll have the car up and running for you tomorrow. Just need to replace the hose."

Deborah thanked him and hung up. Knowing the vehicle could be fixed reassured her, but the possible cause made her sick to her stomach. Had someone tampered with the SUV? The house had no garage, and she parked the car in the driveway. Usually, she locked the doors at night, but she couldn't be positive she did every night. Someone could've opened a door, released the hood latch, and done their dirty work.

If so, was the person the same one who'd sent her the notes?

The problem preoccupied Deborah while she cleaned up the kitchen and loaded her dinner dishes in the dishwasher. Finally, she decided to put the issue aside and focus on her goal of turning Rose Dobson's home—her home, now—into a bed-and-breakfast.

With new determination, she sat at the kitchen table with her list of projects. The remodeling would consume most of her savings and the cash from Rose Dobson's estate left to Deborah along with the house. With January as the opening date, a little over three months remained to complete the project. She needed to keep on task.

Deborah's planning session took her mind off the day's unsettling events—for a while. Eventually, her list completed, she sat back and allowed her thoughts to stray to Milo Jordan. A soft smile crossed her lips as she recalled his friendliness when they first met on the road, and his hospitality later at his home.

Those pleasant images vanished, replaced by the cold, hard look in his eyes when he learned her identity.

Why, oh why did he have to be Carla's brother?

****

Shortly after breakfast the following morning, two employees from Johnson's Auto Repair delivered Debora's SUV. She thanked them for their prompt service and wrote out a check for the bill. She questioned the one in charge again about the possible cause of the problem, but he only shrugged and shook his head.

After watching them leave, she unloaded the rocking chair and end tables she bought at the flea market and hauled them upstairs to an empty room. Then she made a list of errands to do in town. First would be a visit to the police station and then Ripley's Hardware. Last, but certainly not least, was lunch at The Grotto with Lacey Grant.

Deborah became friends with Lacey and Jay Grant when she and Jay taught together at the Wainwright Academy. Sometime during the four years Deborah had been gone, Jay was promoted to headmaster.

Deborah looked forward to her lunch with Lacey, whom she had seen only briefly since her return. Today, they would have time to talk and renew their friendship.

With her list for the hardware store and the envelope containing the threatening notes tucked in her purse, Deborah was ready to leave when the doorbell rang again. She opened the door to find Albert Healy, a young salesman from the Healy Realty and Development Company. Glancing over his shoulder, she saw his blue BMW parked at the curb.

Deborah tensed and gripped the knob. Albert was not someone she wanted to talk to this morning—or, for that matter, at any other time.

Albert peered at her through the screen door. In his early twenties, he had a long, thin face and reddish-brown hair combed straight back from a high forehead. His company uniform of navy blue suit, white shirt, and burgundy tie hung on his lanky form. "Hey, Deborah. Hope I'm not coming by too early."

"I'm on my way out. I don't have time to talk

now."

"Okay, okay. Just wanted to remind you that we're still very interested in purchasing your property." He gave her a wide smile.

Deborah could have guessed as much. Albert had been pestering her to sell out to the Healy Company, owned by his father, Damon. They were developing a neighborhood of homes behind the cul-de-sac and wanted to include her acreage. "I haven't changed my mind, Albert," she said in a firm tone. "The answer is still no." Car keys in hand, she opened the screen door and stepped onto the porch.

Albert's mouth turned down as he stepped aside. "I don't understand why you won't sell. We're making you an offer no one else would refuse."

"As I've told you several times, I'm turning this house into a bed-and-breakfast." Deborah marched across the porch and headed down the steps.

"This town doesn't need another bed-and-breakfast," he argued, close on her heels. "Besides, your old Victorian will be out of place next to our new houses."

"I don't care. I'll plant a border of tall trees behind my house so no one from your development will see my 'old Victorian.'"

"Trees take years to grow."

Deborah ground her teeth together and stepped onto the walkway leading to the driveway and her SUV.

"My father wants to meet with you," Albert said, from not far behind.

Deborah definitely did not want to meet with Damon Healy. He had been on the Wainwright Academy's Board of Directors when she taught there.

Although he had favored hiring her, after Carla's death he was quick to recommend her dismissal. And now he wanted her to sell her property to him? *Of all the nerve.* If she did want to sell, she'd certainly not do so to Damon Healy.

She reached her SUV and unlocked the door. "I'm too busy for a meeting. I want to open my B-and-B by January, and I have a lot to do."

"You'll be sorry."

Hearing his low tone, Deborah turned and stared. His gaze bored into her, and his thin lips were pressed into a tight line. A shiver rattled down her spine. This was a side of Albert she hadn't seen before. "Are you threatening me?" she demanded.

His lips curved into a smile. "Of course not. I just know you'll really be sorry if you don't accept our generous offer. Making as much with your B-and-B will take years."

His sudden change back to Mr. Nice Guy didn't fool her. She lifted her chin. "I'm sticking to my decision."

Still smiling, he nodded. "I'll check with you another time."

Were the Healys responsible for the threatening notes? Deborah wondered, after Albert had left and she was underway in her SUV. They were eager to acquire her property and annoyed that she refused to sell to them. And, of course, they knew all about her involvement with Carla's accident.

If they were behind the notes, how far would they go to get what they wanted?

****

"And you don't know who's behind these notes?"

Detective Leonard Barnet studied Deborah with sober gray eyes.

Deborah shifted in her chair, positioned next to Barnet's cluttered metal desk, debating how to answer his question. She had kept her promise to Milo, but instead of calling the police and having them come to the house, she went to the Fairfield police station instead. So far, she was as uncomfortable here as she would have been in her home. "I don't want to point fingers where I have no proof," she finally said. "Like I told you, a lot of people were upset and angry with me over Carla's death. One of them might be holding a grudge."

Barnet picked up his pen and wrote on his clipboard. When he finished, he tossed down his pen and sat back. "Threats like this are tough to deal with. Even if we know who the perp is, our hands are tied until he takes action."

Deborah leaned back and took a deep breath. The sounds of voices and the ringing of a phone drifted in the open door to his office. "I didn't expect you to do anything."

"Hey, don't write us off just yet." He held up one hand. "Here's what we can do. We'll put an extra patrol on your street, 'specially at night. And I'll let you know if we come up with any fingerprints on the notes. We'll have Mr. Jordan drop by and give us his prints, so we can rule him out. You might want to put some extra security on your house, too."

"I'll give that some thought." She'd have to review her budget first. Deborah grasped her purse and scooted to the edge of her chair.

Barnet pulled a business card from his jacket's

breast pocket and held it out. "Call me if anything suspicious happens."

"I will." Deborah took the card and tucked it into her purse.

So much for that.

Deborah left the police station feeling relieved to have the interview over with but not the least bit reassured. She didn't blame Detective Barnet, though. He would do all the law allowed. Still, if not for Milo's insistence, she wouldn't have come today.

At Ripley's Hardware, after inspecting dozens of samples, Deborah chose a brown stain and yellow-flowered wallpaper for the parlor. By the time she added paintbrushes, thinner, and cheesecloth, she had enough to fill several shopping bags. After loading her purchases in the back of her SUV, she looked up to see a young couple walking by.

The woman stopped and stared. "Miss Kent?"

Recognition dawned. "Piper McCaffrey! Hello." Piper was a favorite student of Deborah's when she taught at the Wainwright Academy. She was also Carla Cassidy's best friend. On the field trip to Rainbow Falls, the two sat together in the back of the school van and later paired up for the leaf-gathering assignment.

Since that day four years ago, Piper had matured into an attractive young woman. She wore dark green slacks and a plaid jacket. A green ribbon held her long, chestnut brown hair at the nape, and a large leather shoulder bag was slung over one shoulder.

"I heard you'd come back," Piper said. "Didn't we, Doug?" She gestured to her companion.

Deborah's gaze shifted to Doug Jaspers. She remembered him as Fairfield High School's star pitcher. In contrast to Piper's professional look, he wore a white T-shirt and blue coveralls with "Bryan's Appliance" sewn across the bib. A red baseball cap advertising "Fairfield Falcons" hid most of his black hair. "Hello, Doug." Deborah offered him a smile.

"Miss Kent."

Doug's icy tone didn't surprise Deborah. He was Carla's boyfriend at the time of her death and outspoken in blaming Deborah for the accident. Still, she winced.

"Are you living in Fairfield again, Miss Kent?" Piper asked.

Deborah nodded. "I am. My guardian, Rose Dobson, left me her house when she passed away. I'm turning it into a bed-and-breakfast. I have lots of work to do." She gestured to her SUV full of supplies and then shut the door. "What are you doing these days?"

Piper pulled the strap of her purse more securely onto her shoulder. "I just started my junior year at Evergreen State. I'm majoring in journalism."

Deborah clapped her hands. "Good for you." Even though she'd taught Piper English for only a couple months, she'd seen her talent for writing. "Do you plan to work for the *Fairfield Monitor*?"

"Probably not. I'm interested in investigative journalism, and there's not much opportunity for that in a small town like Fairfield. I'll have a better chance in a larger city."

"What about you, Doug?" Deborah was determined to be polite, even though during her and Piper's exchange he'd remained sullen.

"Workin' for Bryan's Appliances and managin' the Falcons." He tapped the bill of his cap.

Deborah nodded and smiled. "I've heard Bryan's is a good place to work, and I'm glad to hear you're still involved in baseball."

"Would you like to have lunch sometime, Miss Kent?" Piper asked.

The unexpected invitation both surprised and pleased Deborah. "Why, yes, I'd like that. When would be a good day for you?"

Before Piper could reply, Doug grabbed her hand and pulled her forward. "We don't have time for this, Piper. We gotta get goin'."

Piper shot Doug a frown but obediently trotted along beside him. "I'll call you," she said over her shoulder.

"Please do. My phone number is listed under my guardian's name, Rose Dobson."

As Deborah left the parking lot, she thought about the couple. Piper had been one of the few who had not blamed her for Carla's death. Instead, she remained curiously silent on the subject. At the time, Deborah assumed the shock of losing her best friend accounted for Piper's withdrawal. Now, she wondered if something more lay behind the young woman's silence.

Today Piper acted pleased to see Deborah, yet wary, too. Why? Did her apparent confusion have something to do with Doug Jaspers? Deborah set her jaw. The next time she and Piper met, she would make every effort to find out.

Chapter Four

After completing several more errands, Deborah entered the softly lit Grotto at noon to find Lacey Grant sitting on the banquette in the restaurant's waiting area. The sight of her old friend pushed aside the unsettled feelings from her encounter with Piper and Doug and brought a smile to her lips.

"Hello, Deborah." Lacey stood and held open her arms.

"Good to see you again." Deborah returned Lacey's warm hug.

Lacey straightened, smoothing back a lock of her reddish-brown hair. "You, too, hon."

"You're looking great, as always."

"Thanks. You like my new suit?" She twirled, showing off beige slacks and a lightweight matching jacket that fit smoothly over her slim figure.

"You could be a model."

Lacey laughed. "Missed my calling, did I?"

The maître d' approached, menus in hand, and led them past a burbling fountain and a forest of hanging ferns to a cozy corner table. Shortly after they were seated, a waitress appeared to take their drinks order. Lacey requested a vodka martini and Deborah iced tea. Although Deborah said nothing, she was surprised at Lacey's choice of alcohol for lunch. Not that Lacey didn't drink. She did, but in the past, she'd always waited until cocktail hour to have her martini.

They studied their menus and had both decided on the chicken salad when the waitress returned with their drinks. Orders dispensed with, they raised their glasses and touched them together with a soft clink.

"Here's to your return to Fairfield," Lacey said.

"And to our friendship," Deborah added with a smile.

"Right. Friends forever."

They chatted about Lacey's volunteer work and then about the Grants' sons, Leon and Darren, who attended a military school in a neighboring town. Their salads arrived, and they took time out to sample the food. The chicken had a delicious, tangy dressing, and the greens were crisp and fresh.

"How's Jay doing?" Deborah asked when conversation resumed.

"Oh, he's immersed in his job, as usual."

The sudden weariness in Lacey's voice prompted Deborah to ask, "Lacey, is everything all right?"

"Of course, everything's all right. Don't I have what I've always wanted? A home, children, a successful husband?" She made a dismissive wave.

Lacey sounded like she was trying to convince herself, rather than Deborah. "I guess you do," Deborah said.

"You know my background. I grew up poor. After my father deserted us, I worked in a grocery store to help my mother raise me and my brothers and sisters. Then I met Jay. I saw his potential from the very beginning. I helped him get where he is today."

"You've been a good wife, Lacey. When I heard he was headmaster, I was happy for both of you."

Lacey sipped her martini. "His promotion has, well, put us in a different social class here in Fairfield. Sometimes, I feel a bit guilty being the social butterfly."

"You do a lot of good with your charity work, don't forget."

"Well, I suppose I do." Lacey took a bite of her salad. "But that's enough about me. What's happening with you?"

Deborah rolled her eyes. "I had an awful day yesterday. Wait until you hear." She related her experience with Milo Jordan, adding in an accusing tone, "Why didn't you tell me Carla's brother was living here?"

Lacey ducked her head. "I didn't want to upset you. I never thought you'd meet him by accident."

"Well, it's over and done with now. But he wants me to tell him my version of Carla's accident. Can you believe that?"

"Really?" Lacey widened her eyes. "Do you intend to tell him?"

Deborah sat back and shook her head. "No. I don't want to go through that awful day again."

"I don't blame you. There's no reason to think about the accident any more. You need to get on with your life. Concentrate on turning Rose's house into a B-and-B."

The threatening notes came to mind. Should she tell Lacey about them? Why not? Lacey was her best friend. Now that she'd lost Rose Dobson, Deborah had no one to confide in. "I do want to concentrate on the house, but there seems to be someone who doesn't want me to be here." She brought Lacey up-to-date on the notes.

"That's terrible," Lacey said. "Do you have any idea who it is?"

"Maybe Albert and Damon Healy want to scare me into selling them my property. They want to add it to their housing development. I've told them 'no' several times, but Albert, especially, keeps badgering me."

Lacey broke a roll and spread butter on one half. "I can't believe either of them would stoop so low to make a sale. Can you think of anyone else?"

"Someone who blames me for Carla's death." Deborah lowered her voice. "Doug Jaspers, for one. I saw him and Piper McCaffrey today at Ripley's Hardware. I doubt Piper would threaten me because she never blamed me for Carla's accident. But remember how angry Doug was at me when Carla died?"

Lacey nodded and took a bite of her roll.

"He gave me a cold reception today. By the way, are he and Piper a couple?"

"I believe so. Piper had a crush on Doug when they were in high school. After graduation, he finally got around to noticing her." Lacey wrinkled her nose. "I really can't see them as a couple, though. They're so different."

Deborah frowned. "I didn't know about Piper's feelings for Doug. He and Carla were an item in high school."

Lacey's laugh rang out. "That didn't mean Piper couldn't like him, too. You know how teenage crushes are. But I can't see Doug being mean-spirited enough to send threatening notes, either. What a dilemma." She sobered and leaned forward. "Are you going to the police about the notes?"

Deborah finished chewing a bite of salad. "I hadn't planned to, but Milo insisted. I went to the police station this morning and talked to a Detective Barnet."

"Barnet, hmmm." Lacey pressed a forefinger to her cheek. "I don't think he was here four years ago when Carla…"

"He wasn't. He said he'd look into the files and put an extra patrol on my street. That's about all he can do."

Lacey shrugged. "The notes are probably from some crackpot."

"Maybe, but I hope I don't get any more." Deborah repressed a shiver.

They ate in silence for a couple minutes, and then Lacey said, "We're giving a dinner party next Saturday night. I hope you'll come."

Lacey's invitation chased away Deborah's gloomy thoughts. "A party? Yes, of course I'll come. I've missed the Grants' dinner parties." She had fond memories of having been a guest in the Grants' home on several occasions when she was a teacher at Wainwright.

Lacey smiled, but then her smile faded. "Oh, oh. Maybe you'll change your mind when I tell you Damon Healy and his wife, Ester, will be there. I didn't know about his wanting to buy you out when I invited him and Ester."

Deborah straightened her spine and said in a firm tone, "Don't worry, I can handle Damon Healy."

Lacey raised an eyebrow. "How about Milo Jordan? He's coming, too."

Deborah's enthusiasm drained, and her shoulders sagged. "Oh…so, you're friends. You didn't say so earlier."

"Our association began as a business arrangement, with Milo instructing our students in horseback riding. But then a friendship developed, too."

Did she want to be in Milo's company again? What if he took the opportunity to badger her about the accident? She would be on shaky enough ground without him adding to her distress.

"If you decide not to come, Jay and I will understand," Lacey said.

"I will come." Deborah lifted her chin. "I intend to spend the rest of my life in Fairfield, and I will not hide from anyone."

"Good. I'm glad you've made that decision."

Despite Deborah's declaration, she was nagged with doubts. When they were outside the restaurant, she slowed her steps and turned to Lacey. "Do you think my coming back to Fairfield was the right move?"

"Of course, I do," Lacey said without hesitation. "I, for one, am very glad you did. Jay is, too. Keep your mind on your new B-and-B, and everything will be fine." She gave Deborah a hug. "We'll see you on Saturday, around six."

"I'll be there," Deborah promised.

Twenty minutes later, she returned to her cul-de-sac to see a car parked in front of her home. At first, she thought the visitor might be Albert Healy again—but then she recognized the car as Milo Jordan's. Sure enough, there he was, sitting on her porch steps. Her stomach tightened. He'd come to ask her again to talk about the accident. Well, he'd find out soon enough he'd wasted his time.

As she turned into the driveway, she saw him jump

up and hurry down the steps. He arrived at her car just as she opened the door. Today he wore jeans, a navy wool shirt, and a leather vest. She gave an inward sigh. Why did he have to be so handsome?

"Hello, Deborah." Milo steadied the door while she stepped out.

"Hello, Milo." Deborah kept her voice polite and cool. "What brings you here today?" As if she didn't know.

"I wanted to check on how you're doing. Got your car back, I see. Running all right now?"

"Yes, it's fine." Deborah brushed past him and walked to the back of the SUV.

He shut the driver's door and followed her. "What was wrong with it?"

She made a dismissive wave. "Something about a bad fuel pump. All fixed now." She opened the SUV's trunk and reached for one of the bags.

He lifted out a bag, too.

"You don't have to do that."

"Fuel pump, huh? Okay, but Johnny also said the vacuum hose had a suspicious hole."

The bag forgotten, she stuck her hands on her hips and glared. "If you already know everything about my car repair, why are you asking?"

He shrugged. "Just want to see if you're still in denial."

"Whatever that means." Back on task, she grabbed a sack of painting supplies. "I suppose you know all about my visit to the police station, too."

"Barnet called me to come in and give him my fingerprints. Which I just did. Since I was already in town, I thought I might as well stop by and see you."

39

He shifted his load to one arm and scooped up the remaining bag with the other.

She stepped onto the walk leading to the house.

Milo fell into step beside her. "Looks like you're ready to go to work."

"Yes, I will be very busy." She passed the maple trees and the boxes of geraniums, and climbed the steps to the porch.

"If you need a hand with anything, let me know."

"I'm sure I'll manage," she said in a dry tone. Deborah held her breath as she pulled open the screen door, and, when no note fluttered out, exhaled with relief. Unlike yesterday, she kept her hand firm and steady as she guided the key into the lock, and soon they were inside. "Set the bags on the counter, please," she said when they reached the kitchen. "I'll unpack them later."

He did as instructed.

Then, instead of leaving, as she'd hoped, he tilted his head toward the coffeemaker.

"Is that coffee I smell?"

"I have some left over from this morning, but it's stale by now."

He shrugged. "I don't mind a little stale coffee."

She shook her head and pressed her lips together. "You're making this very difficult."

"What? Getting rid of me?"

"Oh, just sit, and I'll make us some fresh." She gestured to the round table and chairs in one corner. "I guess I can pay you back for your hospitality yesterday. I don't have cranberry bread, though. I haven't had time to do any baking."

"Coffee is fine." He pulled out a chair and sat,

crossing one ankle over his knee.

When the coffee was made and she'd joined him at the table, she searched for a safe topic of conversation. "How's your farm doing?" she asked. "How are the horses?"

His eyes lighted, and he launched into a story about a new mare he'd acquired, a thoroughbred from a prestigious line. "I can hardly wait to see the foals she'll produce."

The story caught her up, and after a while, she could almost forget who he was and the circumstances of their sitting together in her kitchen. Almost, but not quite.

During a lull, he said, "Deborah, about yesterday…"

Clenching her jaw, she put up her hand. "Milo, please, let's not go there."

"No, hear me out. When I got to thinking about all that happened the day we met, I realized I came down pretty hard And, well, I want to apologize."

The sincerity in his voice touched Deborah, and she struggled to keep a grip on her emotions. Falling under this man's spell would be so easy. "Apology accepted," she said. "But that doesn't change my resolve not to talk about the accident. So, in case you planned to ask me again, the answer is still no." Expecting him to argue, she picked up their empty cups and carried them to the sink, signaling an end to their visit.

Instead, he stood, too, and pushed in his chair. "I guess I knew that."

As she led him down the hallway and wondered how to end this meeting, Deborah pressed a hand to her knotted stomach. Would this be the last time she saw him? Would he finally give up and stop badgering her to talk about the accident?

At the front door, he gave her a long, sober look. "We're not finished here, Deborah. I don't give up easily, and you'll be hearing from me again."

Chapter Five

Deborah finished spreading walnut stain on another section of the parlor wainscoting and then checked the clock on the mantel. Four p.m. Except for a brief lunch break, she'd been painting since after breakfast. Any other day, she would take a short dinner break and resume work.

But today was Saturday, and the Grants' dinner party started in one hour. She closed the paint can, cleaned the brushes in a jar of thinner, and went upstairs.

Half an hour later, she trotted back down, dressed in navy slacks, a bright red sweater, and carrying her shoulder purse and navy wool jacket. She was about to slip into her jacket when the doorbell rang.

Who can that be? Albert Healy? If so, she wouldn't answer the door.

She went into the parlor, laid her purse and jacket on a chair, and stepped to the window to peek through the lace curtains. Milo Jordan stood under the glow of the porch light. She shook her head in disbelief. He'd certainly spoken the truth the other day when he said he didn't give up easily. But why show up tonight? Surely, he wasn't here to take her to the party. Without calling first? She considered not answering the door, but ignoring him would only complicate matters later when she had to face him at the Grants'.

Steeling herself for a confrontation, she went to the entry and opened the door. "What do you want, Milo?" she said, her tone brusque.

He grinned and leaned one arm against the doorjamb. "I've come to take you to the Grants' party."

Her heart skipped a beat. "Did Jay and Lacey put you up to this?"

"Nope. My idea."

"I appreciate your thinking of me, but I'll have to say no."

He frowned. "Why?"

"I'm sure you know why. Because I'm not discussing the accident."

"I didn't plan on asking you to."

"Really? That's hard to believe. But, even so, I could still say no."

"But you won't. Not after I've made the trip all the way here to get you."

She shook her head but couldn't help smiling, too. The man did have a certain charm. "You're impossible, but all right. Come in a minute while I get my jacket and purse."

He stepped inside and then stopped to let his gaze rove over her. "You look pretty tonight."

"Flattery won't make me change my mind, but thank you. You look nice, too." More than nice, but she wasn't about to tell him how handsome and appealing he looked tonight in black slacks, a tan pullover sweater, and a black leather jacket.

She put out a hand. "Wait here a minute. I left my purse and jacket in the parlor." She turned and headed back down the hall.

Instead of waiting, he followed her. In the parlor,

he nodded at the newly painted section of wainscoting and then at the cans of stain and jars of brushes sitting in one corner. "You've been busy."

"I have. I've been working in here all day."

"Looking good."

Although pleased by his compliment, she gave only a perfunctory "Thank you."

She picked up her jacket and was about to put it on when he stepped to her side and took it from her hands.

"Here, let me help you with that."

She hesitated, but then turned obligingly and while he held open the jacket, slipped her arms into the sleeves. Was it only her imagination or did his hands linger on her shoulders before he stepped aside?

"All ready, then?" he asked.

She picked up her purse and slung the strap over her shoulder. "Yes. I have directions, too, in case we need them. They're in a different house than they had when I lived here before."

As he pulled shut the door, he shook his head. "No directions needed. I've been there a time or two, and I know the way."

"Lacey said you give the Wainwright students riding lessons."

"I do. And through that I became friends with both Jay and Lacey."

On the drive to the Grants', Deborah expected him to talk about Carla's accident, but he asked about her house remodeling instead, sharing ideas from his own experience. The time flew by, and soon they reached their destination. The Grants' new home was a three-story colonial set amid a grove of pine trees.

Milo pulled up behind the last in a line of cars

parked in the circular driveway and cut the engine.

When Deborah stepped from the car and gazed at the brightly lit house and thought of the party inside, she froze. Since receiving Lacey's invitation, she'd been pep-talking herself, so she wouldn't be nervous about coming. But now that she was here, apprehension pushed to the surface. What if someone mentioned the accident? Would Milo bring it up? Surely not. No matter what he might feel toward her, she did not believe he would intentionally embarrass her. Still, someone else might. Damon Healy, for example.

Milo came to her side. "Are you all right?"

"Of course, I am." She managed a stiff smile.

He grasped her elbow, and they mounted the steps to the colonnaded porch.

A middle-aged woman wearing a plain blue dress covered with a white apron opened the door. She took their jackets and led them into a large, high-ceilinged room resplendent with brocade-covered chairs and sofas, and gilt-framed pictures and mirrors. A cheerful fire crackled in a white marble fireplace. Lacey, Jay, and six other people stood in small clusters, drinking cocktails and eating hors d'oeuvres. Their conversation mingled with the light classical music playing on the stereo console against one wall.

Lacey spotted them and, martini in hand, hurried over.

Deborah took a moment to admire her friend's appearance. She looked stunning in dark brown slacks and a tan silk blouse with long, full sleeves.

"Deborah and Milo." Lacey's gaze shifted from one to the other. "What a coincidence, you two arriving at the same time."

Her arched eyebrows encouraged, if not demanded, an explanation.

"We came together," Milo said.

"Well, isn't that nice?" She sipped her drink. "Come join the group. Oh, Jay," she called. "Deborah and Milo are here."

Jay stood near the mantel talking to several guests. He looked her way, and a smile lighted his angular face. "Deborah!" Placing his drink on a glass-top coffee table, he strode across the room and enveloped her in a hug.

Feeling a rush of affection for her old friend and colleague, Deborah returned his embrace. "Good to see you again, Jay."

Jay released her and held her at arm's length. "Let me look at you. You haven't changed a bit, only grown prettier."

Deborah laughed. "Thank you, kind sir." She wished she could say he hadn't changed, either, but he had. His hair, once a rich brown, was streaked with gray and thinning on top. His cheeks showed deep grooves between nose and mouth, and his eyes, although still a striking midnight blue, reflected a curious sadness.

Still, seeing Jay again lifted Deborah's spirits and chased away her earlier uncertainty about coming tonight. She'd always liked him. He'd been supportive of her as a new teacher and sympathetic after Carla's tragic death.

Jay shook Milo's hand. "Hey, Milo, glad you could make it."

"Nice to be here, Jay."

Jay introduced them to the two couples new to

Deborah, who were Trina and Ralph Thurman, and Elaine and Gary Fox. Both women were associated with one of Lacey's charities. Ralph was a lawyer, and Gary a pediatrician.

"Well, look who is back in town."

Deborah turned and met Damon Healy's cool gaze. Her stomach churned. "Hello, Damon." She kept her voice crisp and polite.

Damon and Milo shook hands, giving Deborah the opportunity to study Damon. He'd gained weight around the middle, and his red hair had more white than she remembered.

Damon's wife, Ester, sidled up and linked her arm through his. "So Rose Dobson left her property to you." She patted her hair dyed to match her black dress.

Deborah nodded. "Yes, she did."

"And you're turning it into a bed-and-breakfast? How…quaint."

Her tone indicated she considered Deborah's plan anything but quaint. Deborah clamped her jaw shut to keep from making a response she might later regret.

"Come on, you two." Jay motioned to Deborah and Milo. "Let's get you set up with drinks."

A few minutes later, sipping her white wine and munching a shrimp hors d'oeuvre, Deborah left Jay and Milo to talk horses and joined Trina Thurman and Elaine Fox. They were discussing their children—they each had two—and complaining about the difficulty of finding good day care.

"I'm hiring a nanny," Trina, a bubbly redhead, declared.

Elaine smoothed the collar of her tailored white blouse and nodded her agreement. "We are, too. Our extra bedroom upstairs would make a great playroom."

Deborah listened politely for a while but then stepped away. She was looking around for Lacey when Damon Healy appeared at her side.

"So, when are you gonna accept our offer on your property?"

Deborah pressed her lips together. "Never. I told you I'm turning Rose's house into a business."

Damon flicked his thick forefinger, as though brushing off a fly. "I don't pay any attention to that. You'll come around."

"You're wasting your time."

"Not likely. Sooner or later, I always get what I want." He turned on his heel and walked off.

Damon's menacing tone chilled Deborah, and she hugged her arms. First, Albert had threatened her, and now Damon. They must be responsible for the notes.

Glancing around, she caught Milo's eye. He was still talking to Jay, but he quirked one eyebrow as though asking if everything were all right. Surprised—and yes, pleased, too—by his perception, she nodded and forced a smile. Then she joined Lacey and the other women who were discussing the landscape painting hanging over the mantel.

Dinner was served in the spacious dining room, where a crystal chandelier beamed over on a table covered with white linen, gold-rimmed plates, and sterling silverware. With graceful waves, Lacey directed them to their seats.

Deborah sat at one end of the table, with Jay on her left at the host's place, and Trina Thurman on her right. Milo sat across from her. She silently thanked Lacey for placing the Healys at the opposite end.

The chicken cordon bleu, mashed potatoes, and grilled asparagus tasted delicious, and Deborah ate with gusto. At one point, she looked up and caught Milo's gaze.

He nodded and smiled.

Warmth filled her, and she smiled back. Perhaps being here together this evening would help Milo to see her in a different light. Maybe then he wouldn't be so hostile.

During a lull in the conversation, Elaine Fox leaned toward Deborah's end of the table and asked, "So, Deborah, how do you come to know the Grants?"

Deborah's shoulders knotted. *Relax. It's an innocent question.* "Jay and I met when we both taught at Wainwright." She hoped her response would end the conversation.

But Elaine raised her eyebrows and said, "Oh? When was that?"

"Ah, four years ago. Right, Jay?" Deborah turned to their host.

Jay speared a bite of chicken with his fork. "Right. I was teaching science and history, and you were making sure the girls used good grammar and read proper literature."

"My mother was an English teacher." Trina Thurman helped herself to more asparagus and then passed the bowl to her husband. "We need good English teachers who will encourage kids to read more. Most kids watch too much TV."

Elaine Fox nodded. "We read a lot to our kids. But I make sure the stories are ones I like, too."

Deborah joined in the ensuing laughter, relaxing now the conversation had moved in another direction.

However, she'd no more than taken the next bite of mashed potatoes when she noticed Gary Fox stroking his beard and frowning. *Oh, oh, what now?*

"You taught at Wainwright four years ago, Deborah?" Gary asked. "Then you must have been there when one of their students died up at Rainbow Falls. They were on a field trip."

"Yes, we moved here about six months afterward," Elaine said, "and people were still talking about it. We were told a teacher was responsible for the girl's death."

Deborah took a deep breath. "Yes, I was here when the accident happened." She swallowed hard and then added, "I was the teacher who took the girls on the field trip that day."

Silence spread over the room like a cloud of poisonous gas. Heartsick, Deborah wished the floor would open and swallow her. Now, she wished she'd never come this evening. She should have known the occasion would be a disaster. She should have known she couldn't come back to Fairfield and lead a normal life.

"The girl who died was my sister," Milo said. "Carla Cassidy."

Deborah winced at the pain she heard in Milo's voice.

"Sorry, Milo." Gary tugged at his beard. "I didn't know."

More silence followed. Deborah dared to glance at Damon Healy. His face wore a sly smile. *He's happy the subject came up. He knows I'm still vulnerable about the accident.*

She shifted her gaze to Milo. His bleak expression

sent her heart plummeting. Well, what else could she expect? Didn't this incident prove Carla's accident would always be between them? She'd been a fool to think they could ever be friends.

"So," Lacey said in a loud voice, "who does everyone think will win the vacant town council seat in November's election?"

Conversation resumed.

After dinner, they moved to the living room for coffee and brandy. No one said any more about the accident.

But whenever two guests put their heads together to discuss something, Deborah imagined they were talking about her. She ached to leave, but didn't want to be the one to break up the party. Everyone would think she was running away out of shame and embarrassment.

Just when she thought her battered nerves couldn't take another minute, Deborah got a reprieve.

Elaine Fox looked at her wristwatch. "It's ten-thirty already. We'd better be going. I told our babysitter we'd be back before eleven."

The others murmured their agreement. Lacey sent the maid for everyone's coats.

Although Milo helped Deborah slip into her jacket, he kept his distance, withdrawing as soon as she had her arms in the sleeves.

Deborah turned to Jay. "Thank you for a lovely evening," she said in a tight voice.

"Glad you could come." Jay patted her shoulder. "We must get together again soon."

"I'd like that."

Lacey burst out with a loud peal of laughter over a

remark from Ester Healy. She waved her martini glass, and the liquid spilled onto her sleeve. A stain spread along the fabric, but she didn't notice.

Jay frowned at his wife. He opened his mouth but then clamped his jaws shut. When he turned back to Deborah, his gracious-host smile was in place, driving the creases deeper into his cheeks. "Why don't you two take Ridge Drive home?" Jay suggested. "That route has a great view of the city."

"We might do that." Milo nodded as he put on his jacket.

Deborah shrugged. She didn't care what route they drove, just as long as it took her home.

Chapter Six

Deborah hoped her nerves would unwind once they left the Grants' home. She'd settled into the car's leather seat and cracked open her window, allowing the cool night air to flow over her hot cheeks and ruffle her bangs. Still, her insides remained coiled as tightly as bailed wire.

She glanced at Milo. His jaw was set; his hands gripped the wheel. He had not uttered a word since they left the party. Well, she wouldn't be the one to break the silence. She had nothing to say that would relieve the situation, anyway.

The evening was a total disaster.

She expected him to ignore Jay's suggestion that they return via Ridge Drive. The route was longer than the way they had come, and undoubtedly he would want to get rid of her as soon as he could. But, to her surprise, Milo turned onto the scenic route, after all.

Any other night, she would enjoy viewing the lights of Fairfield twinkling below. But tonight, sadness filled her. She had looked forward to the Grants' party. Now, she regretted her decision to attend.

Milo threw her another surprise when he pulled off at a viewpoint bordered by a low rock wall. He cut the engine, and its hum soon faded into the night. Leaning his head back against the seat, he gazed out the windshield. "Jay was right," he said. "This is a good view."

"I've always liked it."

Silence.

Deborah shifted in her seat and twisted her fingers together. Why had he stopped here? She wanted to get home, away from everyone. Most of all, away from him.

He cleared his throat. "Deborah, about what happened tonight…I saw how much it hurt you to admit your involvement in Carla's death."

Deborah fiddled with the clasp on her purse. "Telling people always hurts."

"You didn't have to tell them."

"I thought the truth should come from me, rather than from someone else." *Like Damon Healy.*

"It was still a brave thing to do."

He acted like he understood. A glimmer of warmth cut through the coldness wrapped around her heart. "You were upset, too," she said.

"We're both feeling a lot of pain about Carla."

Deborah glanced to her left to see if she could read his thoughts. Moonlight illuminated his expressive mouth and square jaw, but deep shadows hid his eyes. She longed to reach out and touch his arm. Touching might help to ease their grief. To keep from acting on her impulse, she clasped her hands together instead. She let a few moments pass and then heaved a sigh. "Well, the party is over, and I'd better be getting home."

"You're right; we need to go." Milo leaned forward to start the engine.

At her house, Milo walked her to the door. She held her breath as she opened the screen door. When she saw no paper flutter out, she exhaled with relief.

"No more threatening notes?" he asked.

Deborah slipped the key into the lock. "No, thank goodness." She opened the door and then hesitated. Should she invite him in? If she did, he'd probably refuse, perhaps with a lame excuse that would embarrass them both. Then she'd feel even more rejected than she did right now. But when she glanced over her shoulder, she saw an expectant look in his eye.

"Would you, ah, like to come in for a cup of coffee? A glass of wine?" *Please say no.*

"I've had enough wine tonight. Coffee sounds good."

Deborah sighed. So much for rejection. Inside, she took his coat and hung it in the hall closet. "Excuse me for a minute. The kitchen's that way." She pointed down the hall.

"I know. I've been there."

"Oh, of course. The day we met…"

After making sure he headed down the hall, she ran upstairs. In her bedroom, she tossed her jacket and purse on the bed, and then popped into the bathroom to smooth her hair and touch up her lipstick. She shook her head at her mirror image. *Am I crazy?*

Downstairs again, she found Milo in the kitchen filling the coffeemaker's glass carafe with water.

"All we need now is coffee." He turned off the faucet and held up the carafe.

"I'll get it." Deborah took the coffee canister from the cupboard and finished the preparations.

They sat at the table and managed to make small talk while the coffee perked; but after Deborah served the brew, she watched Milo sip his in silence. "Coffee okay?" she asked.

"Great." He took another sip.

"Then…" Her stomach clenched. Something bothered him.

He looked up and met her gaze. "I'm glad you haven't had any more notes, but the two you did receive should be taken as serious threats."

She shrugged. "I reported them to the police. I don't know what more I can do."

"You can tell me who you think might be tormenting you."

Was she that transparent? Or was he grasping? "What makes you think I have any ideas about that?"

He laid a hand on her arm. "Just a feeling. Come on, you can trust me."

His eyes reflected the same concern she'd seen earlier at the lookout. Except for Lacey, and maybe Jay—if Lacey had told him about the notes—no one in Fairfield knew Deborah might be in danger. No one else except the person who sent the notes, of course. Having someone else in her corner, even Milo, would be comforting. "Okay, I do have some ideas. Albert and Damon Healy are pressuring me to sell them my property. They're building a housing development behind my house. They want to expand it to include my place. Come over to the window, and I'll show you."

Deborah stood and walked to the window over the sink. She waited until he was beside her. "You can't see much in the dark, but beyond the hedge at the end of my yard are the backyards of the new houses they're building."

Milo peered out the window. "Yeah, I see the top of a roof. Was this project what you and Damon were talking about so seriously at the party?"

"Yes." Deborah folded her arms and leaned against the counter. "Albert has come by several times to talk me into selling, and Damon waylaid me tonight for the same reason."

"What have you told them?"

"That I'm not the least interested in selling."

They returned to sit at the table. They drank more of their coffee, and then Milo said, "Okay, anyone else?"

"Maybe Doug Jaspers. He was Carla's boyfriend at the time of her accident. Did you know that?"

Milo put down his mug and nodded. "My mother told me she and Doug were dating."

"He was very outspoken in blaming me for her accident. I saw him and Piper McCaffrey the other day outside the hardware store. Piper was friendly, but he was cold. Maybe he wants to avenge Carla's death." She pressed her palms on the table. "There, are you satisfied now?"

Milo shook his head. "You're still holding back something."

Deborah looked away. The seconds stretched into long, tension-filled moments.

Finally, keeping her voice barely above a whisper, she said, "You're right; there is something else about Carla's accident that I haven't told you."

"Tell me now." He leaned forward.

"It's hard to explain, without your having been there that day."

He raised one hand. "We'll go there together, and you can show me."

Deborah drew back and frowned. "Oh, no, I can't go there again."

58

"I'll be with you."

"I know, but—" She clasped her hands together to keep them from shaking. "What am I thinking? Here I am, talking about the accident, when I told you I wouldn't. Don't ask me anymore."

Milo jumped up and came around the table. He knelt beside her chair and took both her hands in his. "Deborah, my sister meant the world to me."

The pain reflected in his eyes made her heart ache. "I'm sure she did."

"After our dad died, Mom, Carla, and I became close. We were there for each other."

"How nice you had such a good relationship," she murmured.

"Yeah, until Mom married again. Then Carla and I got shoved aside. I went off to join the army. I wasn't there to stick up for Carla when she didn't want to go to Wainwright. I wasn't there to be her big brother." He stared at the floor. "I abandoned her."

A lump formed in Deborah's throat. "I'm sorry. I'm so sorry about everything."

"Then go with me up to the falls. Please. Lead me through what happened that day. Look, this isn't only about Carla anymore. You're involved, too. Someone doesn't want you to be here because of what happened. We need to find out who the person is and stop him before his attacks get worse."

"And going up to the falls again will do all that?"

"I don't know." He squeezed her hands. "We have to go there and find out."

Deborah bit her lip. Could she go through the events of that terrible day again? Even for Milo? The sympathy he'd shown her tonight touched her. Maybe in turn she should do as he asked. "All right, we'll go to Rainbow Falls, and I'll tell you what happened."

Milo's eyes lighted. "Tomorrow?"

Fighting back her dread, she sighed. "Yes, tomorrow."

****

The following morning, Deborah paced the floor in the parlor, waiting for Milo to arrive for their trip. She feared she was making a big mistake. Nothing good could possibly come from today's outing to Rainbow Falls. Besides, after he learned the details of that fateful day, he would never want to see her again. Was she willing to put herself through a day of emotional pain just to keep him by her side for a few more hours?

Peering out the window, she spotted his car pulling up at the curb. She hurried to the entry and had the front door open by the time he bounded up the porch stairs.

He stepped inside. "Good morning, Deborah. All ready to go?"

She looked down and shook her head. "No."

"What? Don't tell me you've changed your mind?"

"No, I haven't. I said I would go, and I will." She twisted her hands together and then raised her gaze. "But I'm not ready. I'll never be ready to go through that ordeal again."

Milo placed a hand on her shoulder. "Don't be afraid. I'll be with you every step of the way. I won't let anything happen. I appreciate what you're doing today. Really, I do."

His gentle tone and the sincerity in his dark eyes renewed her courage. "Thanks, Milo. I'll—I'll do my best."

Outside, the sky was a clear, indigo blue, and the

breeze so light the remaining leaves on the twin maple trees barely stirred. Under other circumstances, today would be a perfect day for a ride in the country.

"I've been thinking about how to approach this trip," Milo said, once they were settled in his car and on their way out of the cul-de-sac.

"What do you mean?"

"If it's okay with you, I'd like to start at Wainwright, where you and the students began your field trip."

Another hurdle. A sinking sensation invaded Deborah's stomach. She hadn't been back to the school since her dismissal and had no desire to set foot on the property again. Especially, not today.

"We don't have to go on campus." Milo turned onto the road leading out of town. "I want to retrace the route you took from there."

"You think that's important?"

He lifted one shoulder. "Could be. You never know."

"All right." Knowing she wouldn't actually be on campus eased her tension. "We'll start with the academy."

At Castletown, Milo took a side road leading into foothills still misty with morning dew. The road wound and dipped and climbed through groves of towering trees, silver streams, and green meadows.

Then Deborah glimpsed a familiar tower with a clock face. She drew in a shaky breath. "There's the academy."

Milo nodded and slowed the car. "And a pullout up ahead. We'll stop there." He parked against the low stone wall enclosing the viewpoint.

Deborah opened the door and stepped out. The sun warmed her skin, and the light breeze ruffled her hair. She approached the wall, placing her hands on the rough stones, and gazed down on the school nestled in a valley. Even from this safe distance, emotion filled her. Four years had passed since she'd laid eyes on the school, and yet her time as a teacher there seemed like only yesterday.

Milo came to stand beside her. "Tell me about the campus."

Deborah drew in a calming breath. "The part of the building with the clock tower is for offices. And those L-shaped extensions on either side are classrooms. Mine was on the left, on the second floor." She pointed to the area. "From my window, I could see the stream that winds through the property."

"I see it. And that's quite an athletic field. Covered bleachers, yet."

"Wainwright has the best." Memories crowded her mind, and Deborah allowed herself a smile. "I remember getting ready for the school year to begin. I was excited, yet scared, too. Would the girls like me? Would I be a good teacher?

"I put up a bulletin board featuring characters from Shakespeare's *Hamlet*, which would be their first assignment. I studied my class list and imagined what each girl would be like. After the first day, I took home my first set of papers to grade and showed them to Rose. She was as excited as I was."

"You really liked teaching, didn't you?"

"Yes. I had wanted to be a teacher ever since I can remember."

"Do you know why?"

"Maybe because I always liked being a student. In high school, when my friends preferred to play, I wanted to do my homework. Anyway, at Wainwright, I thought I had fulfilled my dream." Recalling the days she spent at the Academy, few though they were, made Deborah feel warm inside. The halls crowded with the students, the camaraderie of the other teachers, and the exhilaration of teaching. Now, though, her teaching days were over. A sudden sadness chased away the warmth. Hugging her arms, she turned from the wall.

When they were back in the car and underway again, Milo said, "Why don't you tell me how you came to take the girls on the field trip?"

Deborah briefly closed her eyes while organizing her thoughts. "A month after school started, Jay and I discussed taking a group of students on an outing to Rainbow Falls. He planned to give a lesson on the different kinds of trees we would find there. My lesson was on Thoreau's *Walden Pond*."

"But I remember reading in the police report that Jay wasn't with you that day."

"No, he wasn't." She shifted her gaze out the window to a farm where black and white cows grazed in a meadow. "Maybe if he had been, the day would have turned out differently. But Jay called in sick. When I heard, I thought the trip would be cancelled. But Dr. Hammer, who was headmaster, told me to go ahead and take the girls on the outing. He hadn't obtained a substitute teacher for Jay, and he was confident I could handle the students by myself."

"You hadn't planned to take any other adults? Parents? Aides?"

"No, we planned for just Jay and me—and Charlie

Gray, our driver. Our classes were small, only half a dozen girls each."

The "Rainbow Falls Next Exit" sign popped into view, and her stomach tightened.

Milo slowed and turned at the exit. "Go on."

"We all piled into the school van. A couple of absences left only ten girls, including Carla and Piper McCaffrey."

"That still sounds like a handful for one person."

"They were a lively bunch and enthusiastic about the trip. Except for Carla. She appeared to be angry. For most of the trip, she sat with her arms folded and stared out the window." She glanced at Milo in time to see him press his lips together and give a quick nod.

"I'm not surprised. Carla hated Wainwright. She wanted to stay in the public school, to be with all the friends she'd made over the years. Especially her boyfriend, Doug Jaspers."

Deborah nodded. Information she wished she'd had earlier. "So I learned after the accident. At the time, I wasn't aware she hated Wainwright. Her enrolling there had something to do with your mother's remarriage to Ed Cassidy, didn't it?"

"Yes." Milo braked for a sharp curve and then resumed speed. "Ed had a lot of money, and when he married my mother, he wanted Carla to attend Wainwright. Mother supported him, but Carla was furious and threatened to run away. Mother and Ed enrolled her in the school anyway."

"I never knew that. It explains a lot."

"Carla was miserable. Then Mother wrote that Carla had finally found a friend at Wainwright, and she appeared happier."

"The friend must have been Piper McCaffrey." Deborah gazed out the window again. They were climbing through a thickly wooded area. Here and there, the trees parted, revealing orchards and farms nestled in the foothills.

Milo swung the car onto a narrower, road, where thick, towering trees hid the sun. "Rainbow Falls is isolated," he commented. "Why did you choose to go there? Why not Dover Falls? Or Blue River Falls?"

"Jay chose Rainbow Falls because not many autumn colors tours go there. We'd be less likely to be bothered by tourists."

"That makes sense—I guess."

The road ended at a turnaround that included a parking lot. Milo pulled into a space and cut the engine. No other cars or people were in sight.

A lump lodged in Deborah's throat, and her palms were moist with perspiration. Now that they were here, could she go through with this experiment, after all? She turned to Milo. "I don't think—"

"You can do this."

His firm tone discouraged argument. "All right, let's get it over with." She opened the door and stepped out.

At this elevation, the air was sharp and crisp, hinting of colder days soon to come. But the sky was still a deep blue and the sun a bright yellow ball. The distant roar of the falls filled the air. The sound pulled her back to the day four years ago.

Laughing and chattering, eager for fun and adventure, the girls had spilled from the bus.

"There's the path we took." She pointed to the "Rainbow Falls, ½ mile" sign.

Milo took her hand and led her toward the path.

Encouraged and comforted by his support, Deborah trudged along for a few yards. Then, as fear welled up and spread through her, she dug her heels into the dirt. "No! I'm sorry, but I can't go through with this."

"Don't lose your courage now." Milo gently pulled her forward. "Talk to me, tell me what happened."

Relaxing, Deborah sighed. He was right—no use coming this far and then giving up. "Okay. Charlie stayed with the van while I went with the girls. I led the way, with the girls behind me. We walked along this path, like we are doing now."

"Where was Carla?"

Deborah could easily picture the scene in her mind. "She and Piper were at the end of the line. Carla was in better spirits than earlier, and they were whispering and giggling."

The noise of rushing water grew louder, and soon the path opened out to a clearing. A high cliff protected by a chain link fence enclosed the area. To the left was the falls, and to the right a wooden gazebo served as a lookout.

Deborah pointed to the gazebo. "We all gathered there to look at the falls."

She and Milo mounted the gazebo steps and walked to the side overlooking the falls. The silvery water thundered into the canyon below with a force that vibrated the plank floor beneath them. A fine mist floated through the air, landing on Deborah's skin in cold droplets.

The power of the falls never failed to impress her. "Awesome," the Wainwright girls had said as they gazed at the cascading water.

"Have you ever seen a rainbow here?"

Milo's question brought Deborah back to the present. "No, I never have. We didn't see one that day, either, although we hoped to." From the gazebo, Deborah led Milo up a narrow trail that skirted the parking lot. Soon, they reached a meadow of rich green grass sprinkled with yellow wildflowers and surrounded by thick woods.

"We sat under that maple tree and ate our lunch." She nodded toward a tree with enormous girth and limbs full of dark red leaves. "I read aloud from *Walden Pond.* We talked about how we would feel if we lived alone and isolated, as Thoreau had."

Milo put his hands on his hips and surveyed the setting. "Did Carla say much?"

"No, she was preoccupied. I remember she fussed a lot with her hair. It was tied with a ribbon at the nape, but the ribbon kept coming undone. She had such beautiful, thick black hair." *Like yours, Milo*, Deborah wanted to say, but bit back the words.

"She was still in a good mood?"

Deborah shrugged. "More or less. Anyway, after lunch, I gave them Jay's instruction sheet for gathering leaves. I cautioned them about watching out for poison ivy, and they chanted back, 'We know…leaflets three, let it be.'" Deborah smiled at the memory of the girls with their youthful, laughing faces.

"They paired up and went to get their samples. Carla and Piper were partners."

With a narrowed gaze, Milo studied her. "And what did you do?"

Deborah looked away. "I sat under the maple tree and read Thoreau," she finally admitted in a low voice.

"You didn't go with the girls?" He raised his eyebrows.

"Going with them never occurred to me," she said with a hint of defiance. "They were paired up and would be nearby. I could hear their voices, and whenever I looked up from my book, I saw them weaving in and out among the trees."

"Did you ever count heads, to make sure all of them were still there?"

"No, I didn't…But if I had it to do over again, I would have."

"But you don't have the day to do over again, do you?"

Deborah cringed inside. His censure stung more than she cared to admit.

She lowered her eyelids. "No, I don't."

"All right, what happened next?"

"I told the girls to return by two o'clock, which gave them an hour to complete their assignment. At two o'clock, they drifted back. They were laughing and giggling, having a good time. I was happy, too. I considered my first field trip a great success. I was proud to have managed the girls on my own. The trip was almost over—all we had to do was climb back into the van and be on our way."

Deborah bent and idly picked up a red leaf fallen from the maple tree. Thin and brittle, it broke into jagged pieces in her hands. She let the pieces drift back to the ground. "But Piper came back alone. I asked her where Carla was, and she said she had disappeared half an hour earlier. Piper didn't come and tell me at the time because she thought Carla would show up by the deadline.

"I asked the others if they had seen Carla. No one had. We all spread out to the edge of the meadow and called her name into the woods." Deborah nodded at the border of trees. With a little help from her imagination, she could see the girls there now, running back and forth, calling for Carla.

"When Carla still didn't appear, I took the girls back to the van. I told them to stay with Charlie while I searched for Carla myself."

"Why didn't you let them search, too?"

"I didn't dare. What if someone else got lost?"

Milo said no more, and so Deborah went on, her pulse racing. "I left the girls and hurried to the falls, thinking perhaps Carla had gone back there."

The present slipped away. Carla was missing. Deborah must find her. Forgetting Milo, she ran across the meadow and down the path toward the gazebo, as she had that day, calling, "Carla! Carla!" She pounded up the gazebo stairs and across the wooden floor, the sound of her footsteps blending with the roar of the falls. She ran to the railing, looked down—and gasped in horror.

There, on a huge, flat rock at the bottom of the falls, lay Carla. Her arms were out-stretched, her black hair fanned out around her head. As she had that day, Deborah ran from the gazebo. She passed Milo on her way down the stairs. "She's at the bottom of the falls," she said, still juggling the past and the present. "I must go to her."

Deborah headed toward a winding dirt path leading to the bottom of the falls. Pushing aside some low-growing tree branches, she started down. She was about halfway to the bottom when she lurched to a stop.

"What's the matter," Milo asked from behind her.

"I was just about here when I saw something."

He stepped closer and laid a hand on her shoulder. "What? An animal? A deer, maybe?"

"No, something shiny caught my eye."

"What was it?"

"I don't know." She rubbed her forehead. "Everything after that is fuzzy. I remember stopping and looking around, and then running again. And falling. And then nothing until I woke up in the aid car on the way to the hospital."

"Obviously, someone found you."

"Yes, Piper. She left the van and came looking for me. She saw me lying here on the path and Carla at the bottom. She ran back to the van and told Charlie, and he called for help. The police and medics arrived."

"And then?"

"The medics reached Carla, but she was…" A sob caught in her throat and the relived horror threatened to choke her. "She was dead."

Chapter Seven

Milo drove away from the falls, struggling with a mixture of emotions. Since the Grants' party and Deborah's willingness to reconstruct the accident today, he'd mellowed toward her.

But after today, he wasn't sure what he felt. He swung his gaze from the road long enough to dart her a glance. She huddled on her side of the car, shoulders slumped, alternately staring out the window and then at her hands twisted together in her lap. He had the urge to stop the car, pull her into his arms, and comfort her.

No. She was responsible for his sister's tragic accident. While the girls went on their leaf hunt, she sat under the tree reading. Why hadn't she gone on their search and kept track of them all? If she had, perhaps the afternoon would have turned out differently. Clearly, she was negligent. Milo tightened his jaw and kept his foot on the gas pedal.

She'd done as he'd asked today, though. He'd give her that.

Still, he had questions.

He looked at her again, indecision tightening his stomach. Should he let her alone? Or keep digging? Did he have a choice? He cleared his throat. "I've been wondering why Carla took the path to the bottom of the falls. Do you have any theories?"

Deborah shrugged and fingered her purse strap.

"Maybe she wanted to be on her own for a while."

"Maybe. But, could she have sneaked off to meet someone?"

"The police considered that. They asked the other girls if they knew Carla was meeting someone, but no one did."

Milo waved a hand. "What about Carla's boyfriend, Doug Jaspers?"

"The records showed he attended all his classes at Fairfield High on that day."

They passed the "Fairfield City Limits" sign, and Milo slowed. Only a few minutes more and they'd be at Deborah's house. He pressed on. "Maybe a stranger was there, lurking around."

"No evidence of another person's presence was ever found."

Another idea occurred to him. "What about the shiny object you saw? What was it?"

"I have no idea. Whenever I try to remember, my mind goes blank."

"Did you tell the authorities about your experience?"

"I did, but no one thought it was important. They found evidence I'd hit my head on a rock. They decided I'd probably tripped over something and fallen."

"But you think what happened to you is important," he persisted, determined to pin her down.

"A part of me must, because I have nightmares about it. I feel like the memory is stuffed down inside me, but I can't reach in to pull it out."

Milo took one hand from the steering wheel and rubbed his chin. "Memory loss…hmmm. Maybe you have a repressed memory. That happens sometimes when a person sees or hears something so shocking the conscious mind will not accept it."

"Yes, I've heard of that. But I can't imagine what I could have seen that was so awful my mind rejected it." Deborah shuddered and hugged her arms.

Milo fell silent. He had an idea, but would she agree? He'd pushed her hard today. What would she do if he pushed more?

He had to try. He could never live with himself if he didn't follow every possible clue, explore every thread that might lead to solving the mystery of his sister's death.

"I know a doctor in Burlington who works with repressed memories." He turned into her cul-de-sac. "His name is Robert Lawton. I want you to talk to him."

"You really think that's a good idea?"

He waited until he pulled up to the curb in front of her house before answering. "I don't know. But it's all I can think of at the moment that might help us."

"You don't think we should just leave the matter alone?"

He shook his head. "Absolutely not. And you don't, either. You're every bit as troubled as I am."

"You're right. But I'm scared, too. What if I find out something I wish I didn't know?"

He ran his forefinger along her arm. Her skin was warm and smooth. "If what you find out is the truth, then you'll deal with it. The truth is what we're after. Don't you agree?"

Deborah shifted in her seat and gazed out her window.

Should he say more? No, he didn't want to risk

pushing too hard. He waited, hoping she'd agree.

"All right," she finally said. "I'll talk to your doctor."

****

After dinner that evening, Deborah took her cup of tea into the newly painted parlor and sat on the worn brown sofa. She picked up a folder of paint samples lying on the coffee table and leafed through it, intending to choose colors for the upstairs bedrooms.

Instead, she thought about Milo and the disgust on his face when he learned she had not supervised the girls on their leaf hunt.

What were his feelings for her now? Did he hate her? Was he hanging on to their relationship only because she agreed to visit the doctor he recommended?

Her cell phone rang. Welcoming the interruption, Deborah put down the paint samples and answered the call.

"Deborah?" Lacey's familiar voice came over the line. "I wanted to tell you how sorry I am that you were put on the spot last night. But I must say, you handled the situation really well."

The clink of ice cubes sounded in the background. Was Lacey drinking? Concern for her friend tightened Deborah's chest, but she made no comment. Even though they were good friends, she didn't feel comfortable questioning Lacey about her drinking habits. "I appreciate your sympathy, Lacey."

"You and Milo appeared to be getting along okay."

Deborah gave a short, mirthless laugh. "I'm not so sure about that, but we did go to Rainbow Falls today."

Lacey gasped. "You're kidding! I thought you decided not to talk to him about Carla's death."

"I know. But after the party, he caught me in a weak moment, and I agreed to go."

"So what happened at the falls?"

"I went through that day step-by-step I was stressed, but I survived." Thinking about their trip made Deborah's chest ache.

"Did anything special happen while you were there?" Lacey asked.

"I'm not sure what you mean by special; but, no, nothing happened different from the day of the accident."

"What about the shiny object you thought you saw?"

Deborah absently paged through the folder of paint samples. "I told Milo about that and how my memory blanked out. He thinks I might have repressed memory."

"Sounds awfully serious."

"He wants me to see a doctor he knows in Burlington. A psychiatrist named Robert Lawton, who specializes in recovering repressed memories. Milo thinks the doctor can help me find out if I really lost some moments before I fell."

"I can't tell you what to do, of course," Lacey said, "but do you think it's a good idea to keep digging into something so painful?"

Deborah brushed a lock of hair from her forehead. "Probably not, but I told Milo I would see his doctor."

"Well, promise me you'll be careful."

"I will."

"And promise you'll call me or Jay immediately if you need help with anything."

"I promise." Lacey's concern brought a smile to

Deborah's lips. "And, Lacey, I'm so glad we're friends."

"Me, too, honey. Me, too."

****

After a productive day working on her projects, on Tuesday evening Deborah prepared for bed. She went through the house, checking the locks on the doors and windows, and drawing the curtains. In the kitchen, as she reached over the sink to close the blinds, she saw movement outside. Was someone in her yard?

Her heart thumping, Deborah stared out into the dark night, studying the yard. Nothing. All was still. Perhaps she had seen only her own reflection in the window.

Her feeling of unease remained, though, and after turning off the overhead lights, plunging the kitchen into darkness, she crept back to the sink and peered between the blinds' slats. Her gaze swept the yard, settling on the hedge between her property and the Healys' housing development. A shadow shifted. Was someone hiding behind the hedge?

Sure enough, in the next moment a figure slunk from the bushes into the open. He—or she—wore black clothing, gloves, and a knit ski mask with only slits for eyes, nose, and mouth. The person turned toward the kitchen window.

Deborah shuddered and ducked out of sight. Her heart hammered and her throat dried. She let a few seconds elapse and then eased upright. She inched to the window and again peeked through the blinds' slats.

The person was still in the yard. He pranced around, waving his arms and kicking his feet through the pile of leaves she raked earlier that week. Oh, oh, now he aimed toward the back door. Footsteps thudded up the steps and across the porch. The doorknob rattled and shook.

She wanted to scream, "Go away!" but the words stuck in her throat.

She must call 9-1-1. The closest phone was her cell phone in the parlor. She was about to run down the hall, but then the doorknob stopped rattling. Footsteps pounded across the porch. Was he leaving? Or heading for another entrance?

Deborah ran to the kitchen window in time to see the person plunge into the hedge.

Moments later, he burst out the other side and sprinted into a backyard of the housing development. Then he disappeared into the darkness.

She kept a vigil, her senses tuned for the intruder's return. But something told her he wouldn't come back. Not tonight, anyway. All he'd wanted was to terrorize her.

Still, in case he lurked and planned to make another appearance, she'd better have the police investigate. She hurried down the hall to the parlor, snatched up her phone, and punched in 9-1-1.

Ten minutes later, two patrolmen responded to Deborah's call. They listened to her account of the intruder and made a thorough search of her yard and the Healys' property. They found no trace of the mysterious person. Still, the incident left her fearful he might return, and that next time he'd be even bolder.

Chapter Eight

After a restless night, Deborah arose at seven o'clock and fixed a breakfast of oatmeal and toast. While she ate, she glanced frequently out the kitchen window to the back yard. No one hovered around the hedge or on the Healy property. As soon as she finished breakfast, she called the local security company and arranged to have an alarm system installed.

Should she call Milo and tell him about this latest occurrence? No, she couldn't run to him every time she had a problem. She wanted to be self-sufficient.

Although she had plenty of projects, she needed to get out of the house for a while. Piper McCaffrey and her lunch invitation came to mind. Maybe she was available today. Renewing her acquaintance with a favorite student might be just what she needed.

She located Piper's name in the phone book and entered the number on her cell phone. Unfortunately, the call went to voice mail. Deborah was in the middle of her message when Piper came on the line.

"I'm studying at home today," Piper said, "so I'm monitoring my calls."

"Sorry to interrupt you, but I wanted to know when we could get together for lunch."

"Oh, right. I was supposed to call you. Um, how about today? I could use a break from the books."

"Today is perfect. Where do you want to meet?"

"Why don't you come to my apartment? I'll fix us sandwiches and soup. I'd like to show you my place. I'm really proud of the way I've fixed it up."

"That sounds great."

They decided on noon, and Piper gave Deborah directions to her apartment.

After Deborah ended the call, she took out the rented sanding machine. Now that she had something pleasant to look forward to, she'd do a little work in the meantime. She went upstairs to the north bedroom, plugged in the machine, and began sanding the floor. While she worked, she couldn't keep her thoughts from Milo. She hoped he would call today, perhaps with news about her appointment with Dr. Lawton. But, so far, she had not heard from him.

Maybe she should have called him and told him about her mysterious visitor. But what could he do? Thinking about the person dressed in black sent chills down her spine all over again. She wanted to be left alone and to live in peace. Hadn't she paid enough for what happened to Carla?

At eleven thirty, Deborah put away the sanding machine, changed her clothes, and left for her lunch date.

Piper lived in the Fairfield Arms, a newer, five-story apartment building overlooking the Town Commons. The buildings that made up the Commons, including the town hall, the library, and the museum, faced a pleasant park with winding paths, maple and other shade trees, and a pond filled with geese and ducks. Wrought iron benches surrounded a large bandstand with a shake roof and ornate wood trimming.

Today, the sounds of hammering and sawing filled

the air. Workmen constructed a row of wooden booths around the bandstand in preparation for the annual Autumn Festival where local artists and craftsmen displayed their works.

Deborah bypassed the festival area and parked in the Fairfield Arms' guest parking lot. Inside the building, she glanced at the elevator, shuddered, and headed for the "Stairs" sign.

A few minutes later, Piper opened the door to apartment 501 and greeted Deborah. She wore jeans and a red sweatshirt appliquéd with a large blue flower, and leather moccasins. A red ribbon tied her chestnut hair at the nape.

Piper took Deborah's jacket and hung it on the hall tree. "Let me show you around, Miss Kent."

Deborah smiled at Piper's formality. "Call me Deborah, please."

"All right…Deborah. Anyway, I was telling you over the phone about fixing up the place. Everything came either from flea markets or garage sales."

Deborah followed Piper into the living room where high ceilings gave the area a spacious feeling, and a balcony with sliding glass doors added light. "Very nice," she said as she gazed around. "I like the shade of blue you've used for your main color."

"Cerulean blue. I've been learning about color in an art class I'm taking. Are you buying new furniture for your B-and-B?"

"I haven't bought any new pieces yet. I'm doing the same thing you are—flea markets and garage sales. I bought a few pieces at the Castletown Flea Market a couple weekends ago."

"Ah, Castletown. One of my favorite places. The

sofa came from there." Piper gestured to a comfortable-looking sofa set against one wall.

She led Deborah to the balcony, opened the sliding glass door, and motioned her to step out. "This is one of the apartment's best features."

Deborah stepped onto the balcony and looked around. The furnishings included several metal chairs with vinyl cushions, a glass-top table, and a chaise lounge. A pottery planter held a variety of plants and flowers. A fresh breeze drifted from the wooded area across the way, while below a car traveled along a private driveway leading to a residents' parking lot. "How pleasant," she commented.

Standing beside her, Piper nodded. "I love sitting out here. It's quiet and private, and a good place to read or to just think."

The rest of the apartment included a bedroom, a bathroom, and a cozy alcove office with a desk, a computer, and a printer. Piper's special decorating touches made all the rooms attractive.

Over lunch of split pea soup and tuna sandwiches, with a cheerful bowl of red poppies gracing the table, they talked about the series of articles on population growth that Piper was writing for *The Burlington Banner*, where she was interning.

"When do you expect to open your bed-and-breakfast?" Piper asked during a lull in the conversation.

Deborah finished a bite of her sandwich. "By January. I hope. Renovations are not going as fast as I had planned."

"Really? What's holding you up?"

"Some concerns about the accident."

Piper raised her eyebrows. "The accident? You mean Carla's?"

Is there any other accident of importance? "Yes, Carla's."

"Like what?"

Piper's wary tone put Deborah on alert. "I met Milo Jordan the other day."

"Oh, dear, Carla's brother." Piper pressed her hand to her chest.

"We met by chance when my car stalled on the road to Castletown. I was returning from the flea market I mentioned earlier."

Piper nodded and dipped her spoon into her soup. "I know the route. It's the same one I take."

"Milo was out horseback riding and stopped to help me. He took me to his house and called a tow truck. We were getting along quite well until he found out who I am."

"What a coincidence you two should meet like that."

"Yes, the occurrence was a shock to both of us." She recalled how she'd wanted to escape his presence. "Anyway, he wanted to hear my account of what happened at Rainbow Falls. As you can imagine, I didn't want to talk about the accident. But, during the following days, he finally convinced me that if I did, both of us might benefit."

Piper's mouth turned down. "How could reliving that awful day possibly help you?"

Deborah sat back, her soup and sandwich forgotten for the moment. "I've suffered a lot of guilt over Carla's death. You can't imagine how much."

"Oh, I think I can." Piper bit her lip and looked

away.

"Milo has some feelings to work through, too. I thought a trip to Rainbow Falls might help us both to heal."

Piper dropped her soupspoon, and it clattered onto her plate. "You didn't! How could you possibly put yourself through such an ordeal?"

Well, that's a bit extreme. Deborah took a deep breath. "The trip took a lot of courage and heartache, but I managed."

Piper shook her head and picked up her spoon. "I have never gone back. I don't think I ever will again. Every moment of the tragedy is etched forever in my memory."

"The day is burned into my memory, too—most of it."

"What do you mean, 'most of it'?" Piper narrowed her eyes.

"You remember that when I was trying to reach Carla, I somehow fell and lost consciousness."

"Of course, I remember. I was the one who found you."

"Yes, for which I will be forever grateful." Deborah gave Piper a wan smile. "But, oddly enough, I lost a few moments before I fell."

Piper frowned and shook her head. "I don't understand."

"I don't, either. That's the problem." Deborah fiddled with her napkin. "Those moments are missing from my memory. Milo thinks maybe I saw someone or something so shocking I repressed the memory. You've heard of repressed memories, haven't you?"

"I did a paper on the subject for a psychology

class." Piper straightened her shoulders. "I interviewed people on both sides and came away not sure whether I believe in the phenomenon or not."

"I know what you mean. The theory is controversial. But, I was wondering, Piper, did you see anyone that day who wasn't part of our group?" Anticipating Piper's answer, Deborah leaned forward.

Piper drew back. "Don't you remember that at the inquest I said I saw no one else? Are you suggesting I lied?" Her voice rose.

Fearing she'd gone too far, Deborah spread her hands and shook her head. "No, of course not. I thought you might have remembered something new since then. I probably shouldn't have brought it up, but I must admit I've been caught up in Milo's suspicion that Carla's death may not have been an accident."

"That's preposterous." Piper stuck out her chin. "Of course, it was an accident. Listen, Miss Kent...Deborah...if I were you, I'd forget about Carla's death and get on with my life."

Deborah pressed her lips together. "I can never forget her and what happened that day. And as for getting on with my life, I'd like to, but that's difficult right now."

"Then perhaps you shouldn't have come back to Fairfield, after all."

Piper's cold tone sent shock waves through Deborah. Still, she straightened her spine and met the young woman's gaze. "But I did come back. And, no matter what Milo and I discover about Carla's death, I intend to stay in Fairfield. No one will change my mind about that."

On her way home, Deborah thought about Piper's

insistence about reporting everything she knew about the accident at the inquest. Then the coldness in her voice when she suggested Deborah shouldn't have returned to Fairfield. Could Piper be involved in the attack? Could she have sent the notes and tampered with Deborah's car? Could she have been last night's stalker?

Whatever the answers might be, instinct told her Piper was hiding something.

****

Two days later, Deborah spent the afternoon upstairs in the north bedroom preparing a dresser for refinishing. Needing a break, she put down her dust rag and stepped to the open window. Cool autumn air floated in, along with sounds of hammering from the Healys' housing project. Deborah frowned. She hoped the crews would be finished by the time her B-and-B was ready to open. She wanted her guests to have peace and quiet, not noise and confusion.

Her cell phone rang. She pulled it from her slacks' pocket and saw Milo's name on the screen. Her heart beat faster. Several days had passed since their trip to Rainbow Falls, and she'd been wondering what he was up to.

"I contacted Bob Lawton," he told Deborah after they'd exchanged greetings. "The doctor I told you about?"

"Right. Can he see me?" She held herself rigid, waiting for his answer. Part of her hoped for a "no," while another part hoped for "yes."

"On Monday at two in the afternoon. I hope you're free."

Deborah let her shoulders relax. "I am."

"Good. I'll pick you up at one. That will give us plenty of time."

"You don't need to go with me." Deborah waved her hand. "I'm perfectly capable of going alone."

"I know you are. But since I suggested you see him, I'll go with you."

The exaggerated patience in his tone sent a clear message. She should know by now that if he wanted to accompany her, he would. "All right, all right."

"Is everything okay? You seem tense. Have you received any more threatening notes?"

Deborah bit her lower lip. Should she tell him about the intruder? Keeping the incident from him wouldn't be fair. "No notes...but someone tried to get in the house a few nights ago."

"What? Tell me what happened."

Deborah paced the floor as she related the incident.

"Why didn't you call me?" he demanded.

"I didn't want to bother you. I called the police, though. You should be happy about that."

"I am, but I would have appreciated a call, too. Now, I'll worry about you staying there alone."

She smiled at the sincerity in his voice. "Don't. I'll be fine. I think the person only wanted to scare me. If he really wanted to get in, he would have."

"That's supposed to make me feel better?"

"Don't worry, Milo. Please. Besides, tomorrow an alarm system will be installed."

"Good. I was going to suggest that."

They talked for a few minutes longer, and then he said, "I'll say good-bye now. See you Monday. But promise me you'll call if anything else happens. We're in this together, Deborah, whether you like it or not."

We're in this together. Milo's words echoed in Deborah's mind after they hung up. She shouldn't read too much into his remark, though. He was interested in her only for what she could help him learn about his sister's death. When that business was concluded, they would go their separate ways.

No matter how much she might long for a relationship, she could never have one with Milo. Carla and her tragic death would always stand between them.

****

The following morning, the security company arrived and installed an alarm system, which included arming all the doors and windows, motion detectors, and monitoring. After they left, while Deborah sat at the kitchen table reviewing the instruction booklet, she received a call from Lacey.

"Checking in to see how you're doing," she said.

"Pretty good, considering what happened the other night."

"What? Tell me."

"Someone wearing a ski mask was prowling around the back yard. He came up on the porch and tried the doorknob. Luckily, I'd locked the door earlier." Deborah stood and walked to the window over the sink. She gazed out, and the memory of the menacing figure sent a shiver down her spine.

Lacey gasped. "Oh, Deborah, that's awful. You must have been terrified. I know I would've been."

"Being stalked like that wasn't fun. After he left, I called the police. They came and looked around but didn't find anyone. And now I have an alarm system." Her gaze traveled to the newly installed keypad by the back door.

"That's good to hear. But even with an alarm, are you sure you want to stay there?"

"Yes, I am. I will not let a…a *prankster* scare me away." Deborah made a fist and pumped the air.

"I like your determination, hon, but I have to say, you've got me worried."

"Thanks for your concern, Lace, but I'll be fine." The alarm system made her feel secure.

"What about the doctor Milo wants you to see?"

"Dr. Lawton. I have an appointment at two o'clock on Monday."

"I hope some good comes of your visit."

"Me, too."

After lunch, Deborah returned the sander to the rental shop. She paid her bill at the counter and was tucking her receipt into her purse when she spotted Doug Jaspers exiting the manager's office. Considering the cold reception he gave her when he was with Piper, Deborah considered avoiding him today. However, before she could turn away, she was spotted.

"Hey, Miss Kent!" His long-legged stride brought him quickly to her side. "Been wantin' to talk to you. Was gonna call."

Deborah's shoulders tightened. Why would he want to call her? "What about?"

"Not here. We'll talk outside." He gestured to the door.

Deborah didn't like his demanding tone. Still, they were in public. What could happen? And, maybe she'd learn something useful. "All right."

Outside, Doug led them several yards away from the building. Then he stopped and stood in front of her, blocking the way to her car.

His blue eyes glinted like chips of ice. A little shiver skittered down her spine. Maybe talking to him wasn't such a good idea. "What's on your mind, Doug?"

"Piper told me you two had lunch the other day. She was really upset when you accused her of lyin' about Carla's accident."

What a gross twist of the facts. Putting aside her fear, Deborah stood tall and lifted her chin. "I didn't accuse Piper of anything. I merely asked if since the accident she had remembered anything new."

Doug propped his hands on his hips. "Why would she remember somethin' since then? That don't make sense."

Deborah thought about mentioning the theory of repressed memories, but she decided to keep that to herself. "I'm sorry if our conversation upset Piper. I hope she and I can be friends."

"I suppose that's up to her."

"I know how much Carla's death upset you, too, Doug. You and Carla were going together at the time, weren't you?" While waiting for his response, she studied his expression.

Doug shoved his hands in the pockets of his coveralls. "We went out a few times."

"You were at your school when she had her accident, isn't that right?"

He furrowed his brows. "Course, I was. Why'd you bring that up?"

"Carla's brother, Milo Jordan, and I are looking into her death. Milo thinks maybe she was meeting someone that day."

"And you think it was me." He poked his thumb at

his chest. "What a crock. I didn't know what happened until later that afternoon when I turned on the TV news."

So far, all his answers agreed with what she already knew. Maybe probing beneath the surface would reveal something significant. "Doesn't Carla's going off alone seem strange?"

Doug snorted. "Carla hated Wainwright. Didn't surprise me she disobeyed your orders and left the group. But so what? You're still responsible for what happened." He stepped closer and stuck his finger in her face.

Deborah winced but held her ground. *Yes, Doug, be sure you let me know I'm to blame.* "Well, again, I'm sorry Piper's upset."

"Okay. But knock it off, will ya? If you want to live here, let the past—and Carla—rest in peace."

He wheeled around and strode toward a white Bryan's Appliance van. He climbed in and roared from the parking lot.

Deborah stared after him. Doug Jaspers was an angry young man. Why? Because Deborah had upset Piper? Or for some other reason?

Chapter Nine

"Now, I've got both Piper and Doug upset with me," Deborah told Milo on Monday morning. They drove along the road to Burlington, on the way to Deborah's appointment with Dr. Lawton. She'd told him about her lunch with Piper and the tense scene with Doug outside the rental store. "Maybe I'd better leave well enough alone, as they suggested."

Milo took his gaze off the road long enough to give her a frown. "And continue to be harassed? I don't think so. We need to find out who wrote the notes and who stalked you the other night, even if it does alienate a few people."

"You're right." Deborah sighed. "I'm glad you keep reminding me."

"Don't worry. I'm a bear when I want something." Milo set his jaw.

"So I've noticed." Deborah allowed a hint of sarcasm to creep into her voice, and then held her breath.

But Milo said no more on the subject.

A few minutes later, they arrived in Burlington. Milo parked the car, and they entered the five-story Cobb Building.

"Robert's on the fourth floor," Milo said when they were in the marble-floored lobby. "The elevator's straight ahead on the left."

Deborah stopped walking. "Would you mind if we took the stairs?"

He gave her a teasing grin. "Looking for some extra exercise?"

"Not exactly. I avoid elevators. When I was in college, I was stranded in one for five hours."

His grin changed to a grimace. "Ouch. That couldn't have been much fun."

"Especially when you're claustrophobic to begin with. So…stairs?"

"Of course." He grasped her elbow and guided her to the stairway.

At the doctor's office, the receptionist, an attractive redhead with a ready smile, gave Deborah a new patient form to fill out. After completing the form, Deborah perched on the edge of her chair and knotted her hands in her lap.

Milo reached over and caught her hands. "Relax, Deborah."

Their gazes meshed, and warmth spiraled through her. If only they had met under different circumstances.

At last, the door to the doctor's office opened, and Dr. Lawton stepped out. He was about six feet tall, with black hair graying at the temples. Dressed in navy corduroy slacks and a gray, V-neck sweater, he looked more like a college professor than Deborah's idea of a psychiatrist. Some of her nervousness seeped away.

Dr. Lawton smiled, and then his gaze landed on Milo. He stepped forward, his arm outstretched. "Milo, good to see you again."

"You, too, Bob." The two men shook hands, and Milo nodded at Deborah. "This is the young lady I told you about. Deborah Kent."

Deborah and the doctor exchanged greetings.

Dr. Lawton gestured to the open door behind him. "Come on in my office, and let's get started."

Deborah took a step forward and then stopped. Her heart thudded. Did she really want to go through with this appointment?

Milo placed a hand on her arm. "You'll be okay, Deborah. You're in good hands."

She gave him a weak smile, took a deep breath, and entered the doctor's private office.

In addition to the customary desk, computer, and other office furnishings, the room included an overstuffed sofa and several easy chairs grouped around a fireplace where fake red and yellow gas flames licked at artificial logs. Perhaps the décor was meant to put a patient at ease, but Deborah's nerves tingled and her throat felt dry.

"Have a seat, Deborah." The doctor gestured to the sofa. He picked up a clipboard from his desk and sat in one of the easy chairs. "Tell me a little about yourself and why you're here. Milo sketched in a few details, but I'd like to hear them from you."

Deborah took a deep breath and launched into her story.

Dr. Lawton took notes, occasionally interrupting to ask a question.

"I'm here to see if I have repressed memory about that day," she said when she finished. "And if I do, to discover what happened during the forgotten time."

Dr. Lawton put down his pen and made a tent with his long fingers. "The theory of repressed memory is controversial among mental health specialists."

"I'm aware of that. So, if you don't think this will

do any good…"

He tilted his head. "You don't want to be here very much, do you?"

Deborah spread her hands. "I admit my coming here was Milo's idea. But I do want to know exactly what happened as I ran down the path that day. Did I really see something shiny? And if so, what was it? And I do want to stop whoever's harassing me."

"Then listen to what I have to say about repressed memory. I've worked with patients who have recovered memories that proved to be true. And I've had patients whose so-called memories had no basis whatsoever in reality."

Deborah frowned. "They mistook imagination for memory?"

"Apparently. Anyway, I'm sensitive to the criticism that a therapist may unintentionally lead a person to believe he's recovered a lost memory. To lower the risk, I proceed very carefully."

"I understand."

Dr. Lawton leaned forward and clasped his hands. "However, I believe therapy is worth a try. My main method is hypnosis. For you to be regressed, you must be willing."

Deborah stared at the fireplace, where the gas flames made the same colorful patterns, over and over. "I've come this far, and so I'll go ahead."

"Good. Do you want to begin today?"

She bit her lip but then nodded. "If there's enough time left."

Dr. Lawton pushed back his sweater sleeve and looked at his wristwatch. "Officially, we've about fifteen minutes, but I can give you an extra ten on top of that. We'll try a light hypnosis, to see how you handle the procedure."

"All right." Even as she agreed, Deborah had the sudden urge to jump up, run from the office, and make Milo take her away. She wanted to find out the truth, yes—but, whenever she took a step in that direction, a strange fear seized her. Dr. Lawton was speaking again, and she struggled to focus on his words.

"First, I want you to keep in mind that nothing you encounter while you're under hypnosis can hurt you. You're going back to that day as an observer. Okay?"

Deborah nodded.

"Get comfortable but keep your back straight. Rest your hands in your lap."

Deborah shifted until her spine pressed solidly against the sofa cushions. She placed her hands, palms up, in her lap. Her hands were hot and moist with perspiration, and the sudden exposure to air washed her skin with a strange coolness.

"Close your eyes and take a deep breath."

Deborah lowered her eyelids and drew in a breath, feeling her chest expand and then deflate as she exhaled.

"Now, breathe normally, but concentrate on your breath as it flows in and out."

She breathed in and out, again and again, until she established a rhythm. The sense of her surroundings faded, leaving her in a vacuum.

"I want you to visualize yourself standing at the top of a flight of stairs." Dr. Lawton's voice penetrated the void. "Tell me when you're there."

Deborah imagined a flight of stairs, not connected to anything, just there. "Now."

"All right, step by step, descend the stairs. As you go down, you're also going back in time. When you reach the bottom, you will be at Rainbow Falls on the day of the accident."

Rainbow Falls. The day of the accident.

As though she were watching another person, Deborah saw herself going down the stairs, step by step.

"Tell me when you get to the bottom," Dr. Lawton instructed.

After a few moments, Deborah murmured, "I'm at the bottom now."

"Good. Now, tell me what happened on that day. Take your time, and give me as many details as you can remember."

Deborah related the events of the field trip. When she came to the part where she ran down the path to reach Carla, she suddenly cried out, "Oh, no! I feel sick, like I'm going to throw up. I want out of here!"

"Take a deep breath and let it out slowly," Dr. Lawton said in a quiet voice. "Remember, nothing there can hurt you now."

Deborah swallowed against the lump in her throat and then gulped in air. Still, nausea gripped her. Clutching her stomach, she doubled over and clenched her teeth. "I want out of here."

"All right. I want you to turn away from whatever is making you sick and walk back to the steps. Tell me when you're there."

After a minute or so, Deborah straightened to a sitting position. "I'm there."

"Start climbing the steps. Keep your breathing even and relaxed—in, out, in, out. As you climb, time is passing, and you are returning to the present. When you reach the top, open your eyes."

The stairs seemed never-ending, but at last, she reached the top. She opened her eyes. Dr. Lawton came into focus.

He leaned forward, watching her. "Hello, there. How do you feel?"

Deborah managed a slow smile. "I'm okay, but the process didn't work, did it? I got stuck, just like I do when I try remembering without being under hypnosis. I didn't see anything shiny, either. Maybe that means I only imagined I saw something that day."

Dr. Lawton shook his head. "Don't worry about the treatment not working this time, Deborah. Recovering a lost memory may take several sessions."

She looked down at her hands still clasped in her lap. "I hoped today would be my only visit."

"I understand. But keep in mind that if a memory exists to be recovered, it might return to your consciousness at any time. Recovery doesn't have to be while you're under hypnosis. In fact, sometimes a visual clue will prompt a memory to return."

She met his gaze. "A visual clue?"

"Yes, you'll see something you also saw during the repressed event, and the memory comes rushing back. Depending on what the memory is, the result could be traumatic."

"Oh, great." Deborah rolled her eyes. "All I need is another trauma."

"You have my promise that I'll make the recovery—if there is to be a recovery—as smooth as I can." Dr. Lawton stood and gestured toward the door. "Alma will schedule your next appointment."

Deborah's breath quickened, and she twisted her fingers together. "Oh, Dr. Lawton, please don't take this personally—you've been very kind—but I don't know whether or not I want additional sessions."

Dr. Lawton smiled. "I understand, and I'm not pressuring you to continue. The decision is entirely up to you. But I do hope to see you again."

"I'll let you know what I decide."

****

On the drive back to Fairfield, Deborah filled in Milo on her appointment. "Dr. Lawton hypnotized me, but I still couldn't recall those lost moments."

Milo took his gaze off the road long enough to give her a reassuring smile. "Don't be too concerned. You may have to try several times before you're successful."

"That's what he said, but I'm worried that more sessions will be a waste of time."

"Have patience, Deborah. I'll take you to the appointments, so you can relax beforehand. And after...like now. Why don't you sit back and enjoy the ride home?" He nodded toward the window where the sunny countryside rolled by.

Deborah leaned back in the seat and managed to take Milo's advice—until they turned into her cul-de-sac and she saw a familiar blue car parked in front of her house. Then her nerves knotted once again.

"Looks like you have company." Milo pointed to the late-model luxury sedan.

"That's Albert Healy's car. Damon's son. Remember, I told you they want to buy my property and expand their housing development."

"I certainly do remember. We'll see what he's up to." Milo pulled to the curb behind Albert's car, and he and Deborah stepped out.

Albert emerged from his car and approached Deborah. As usual, he wore a navy blue suit, white shirt, and burgundy tie. "Hello, Deborah." A smile widened Albert's long, thin face.

"Hello, Albert." Deborah kept her tone crisp. "This is Milo Jordan," she added, gesturing to Milo.

The two men shook hands.

Albert turned back to Deborah. "I stopped by to see if you changed your mind about talking to my father."

She shook her head. "No, I haven't. In fact, I saw him at a party recently and told him I wasn't interested in selling my place. Didn't he inform you?"

Albert made a dismissive wave. "He might have. But I wanted to check with you, again, anyway."

"What made you think Deborah might have changed her mind?" Milo stepped closer to Deborah.

Albert widened his eyes. "Why…nothing special."

"Deborah has told you repeatedly she doesn't want to sell, so why are you still hanging around?" Milo stuck out his chin.

Albert held his ground and kept his head high. "I don't call stopping in occasionally to check on a potential client 'hanging around.'"

Deborah huffed. His visits had been too frequent to be considered "occasional."

Milo continued. "Yet, when you found she wasn't here today, you waited. You hung around."

Seconds ticked by while the two men stared at one another.

Finally, Albert broke eye contact and turned to Deborah. "I'll come back another time."

He climbed in his car and sped off.

Milo folded his arms and narrowed his eyes at the retreating car. "I don't like that guy."

"I don't particularly like him, either. But I suppose he's just doing his job."

"He can do it elsewhere. Plenty of other properties are available in Fairfield. He doesn't have to pressure you to sell yours."

Although Deborah considered herself perfectly capable of handling the likes of Albert Healy, she found Milo's protective gesture sweet and touching. "Thanks for putting in a word." She headed up the walk to the front porch.

"You're welcome." Milo fell into step beside her. "He looked like he needed somebody to get in his face, and I'm good at that—when I want to be."

She glanced sideways, caught his grin, and laughed. "You are good at that." Then she thought about Albert again and her laughter faded away. "Do you think he is the one who's harassing me?"

"He could be, but we have no proof. All we can do is keep an eye on him."

"Would you like to come in for a while?" Deborah asked when she reached the door.

Milo looked at his wristwatch. "I'd better not. I need to get back to the farm."

"That's right, you do have a farm to run." Deborah took her key from her purse.

Milo laid a hand on her shoulder. "Hey, I didn't mean to sound as though I didn't want to spend more time with you."

Deborah's pulse quickened. "You don't need to explain."

Milo grasped her shoulders and turned her around.

Their gazes met, and heat flew back and forth between them. Milo cupped her chin and lowered his mouth to hers in a soft kiss. Then he deepened the kiss, locking his arms around her and pulling her close.

With a sigh of surrender, Deborah wrapped her arms around Milo's neck and returned his kiss. Being in his arms sent warmth spiraling through her.

Long moments passed before he finally drew away. "Oh, Deborah," he whispered against her hair, "I just had to see if kissing you was as good as I wanted it to be."

"Was it?"

"No."

Deborah stiffened and jerked back her head. "No?"

"It was better." He laughed and then sobered. "Sorry, I shouldn't tease you, especially when you've had such a rough day."

"You can tease me. I'm not as fragile as you may think." Not quite true. Where he was concerned, she was as fragile as glass.

He hugged her again. "Maybe I'll take you up on your invitation, after all."

Now, after the kiss, she had second thoughts. If he came in, would they start kissing again? And if so, where would that lead? More intimacy would be dangerous, considering they had no future together.

Placing her hands on his chest, she gently carved some distance between them. "You've already made your decision. I don't want to be responsible for you neglecting your duties."

"But—"

"Please, Milo."

Milo took a deep breath and exhaled. "You're

right, I should go." He pulled his car keys from his jeans' pocket. "You take care."

"I will. You, too."

With a heavy heart, Deborah watched Milo climb into his car and drive away.

Chapter Ten

During the next week, Deborah refinished another bedroom dresser and bedstead and hired a craftsman to replace damaged tile in the bathroom. An electrical crew brought the wiring up to code. The sudden spurt of progress raised her spirits. Her dream of turning Rose Dobson's home into a bed-and-breakfast was well on the way to becoming reality.

On Friday, Deborah received a thick envelope in the mail. The return address showed a Fairfield Post Office box but included no name.

She took the letter into the parlor and sat on the sofa. Slitting it open with her letter opener, she removed two single-spaced, typewritten pages, and a smaller sealed envelope. The typewritten pages proved to be a letter from Piper McCaffrey, as evidenced by her signature at the bottom of the second page.

What did Piper have to say that she could not tell Deborah over the phone or in person? Something to do with Carla's accident? Eager to discover the answer, she turned to the letter's first page and read:

"Dear Deborah,

I hope you don't think I'm a coward for writing this letter instead of telling you what I have to say. At our lunch the other day, you asked me if I remembered anything new about the accident. I told you I have not, and that is the truth.

What I didn't tell you is that I do have information about that day that I knew from the beginning, yet shared with no one. This has weighed heavily on me for the past four years, probably as much as your guilt has weighed on you.

On the way to Rainbow Falls, Carla told me Doug Jaspers wrote her a note asking her to sneak away from our group and meet him on the path to the bottom of the falls. All sorts of hiding places are there where they could spend time together.

I don't know if she actually met Doug. I never saw him there, and that's the honest truth. But because I had a crush on Doug at the time, I kept quiet.

You're probably wondering how Doug could have been with Carla when attendance records indicated he was at school. I can't prove how he accomplished that, but I do know his first class after lunch was a geology lab, in which a buddy of his took roll for the teacher.

Maybe Doug asked his buddy to mark him present. I know he did this on other occasions when he and Carla met on the sly.

After the accident, I went through Carla's belongings—we were roommates, you know—and I found the note Doug had written. I've kept it all these years.

I've never confronted Doug with my knowledge. Now that I know him better, I realize he is not the man for me. Our interests and lifestyles are too different to ever be compatible.

Anyway, here's the note. Maybe you'll know what to do with it. Should the time come when I'm expected to verify all this, I may just deny everything.

Honestly, Deborah, I do want the truth about

Carla's accident to be revealed. You're right—her tragic death hangs over us, unfinished business to be put to rest before we truly can get on with our lives.

I am following up another lead, prompted by something Carla gave me shortly before she died. I won't say any more until I've discovered something conclusive. If I do, I'll let you know.

Whatever you do, be careful!

Piper McCaffrey"

Deborah stared at the letter, her mind racing with the new information, considering how the situation had changed, if at all. Then, coming to her senses, she laid aside the letter and picked up the sealed envelope. She slit it open and reached in to pull out the enclosed paper. Not wanting to put her fingerprints on the note, she jerked away her hand. She went to the bathroom, retrieved a pair of tweezers, and used them to pull out the paper. With awkward movements, she unfolded it with the tweezers and held it flat so she could read the message:

"Hi, Carla,

I can get away from school on Friday. Meet me on the path to the bottom of the falls. I'll be there about 12:30.

Doug"

Deborah had no way of knowing if the note was authentic, but the possibility of Doug being at the falls the day of the accident added a new perspective. Had Deborah seen Doug as she ran down the path? Perhaps he had threatened her, frightening her so badly she repressed the memory.

Doug might now be afraid Deborah would somehow recover her memory and tell the authorities.

Had Doug tampered with her car, sent her the threatening notes, and skulked around her yard in a ski mask?

She needed to share Piper's letter and the note with Milo. Perhaps he would know what they should do next. She picked up her cell phone, selected his number, and exchanged greetings with the housekeeper.

"He's gone to Edington," Katie said, "to see about some horses."

"Please have him call me as soon as he returns." Deborah ran her fingers through her hair.

Seven p.m. rolled around before Milo returned her call.

"Can you come over?" she asked. "I have something to share with you."

"I'll be there in half an hour."

Milo arrived as promised, and the welcome sight of him made her senses hum. She wished this were a social call, instead of one where they needed to discuss the subject so painful to them both.

She led him into the parlor where she had a carafe of coffee and mugs ready. She waited until he was seated on the sofa and had taken a few sips of coffee and then handed him Piper's letter.

He raised his eyebrows. "What's this?"

"A letter from Piper McCaffrey. I'll let you read it for yourself."

When she saw he was finished with the letter, she took her tweezers and removed Doug's note from the envelope. "I thought I'd better not add any fingerprints." She spread the note on the coffee table.

Milo read Doug's note and then looked up, a frown creasing his brows. "Hard to believe Piper would withhold this from the authorities."

"At the time, she had a crush on Doug. She didn't want to think he could've been involved with Carla's death. She wanted to protect him."

"And now she's studying to be an investigative reporter?" He folded his arms and shook his head.

They both fell silent.

Then Milo leaned forward and tapped his forefinger on the coffee table next to where the note lay. "So, was Doug there, or wasn't he?"

Deborah clasped and unclasped her hands. "Maybe we'll never know for sure. If he's confronted with the note, he could always deny he wrote it on that occasion. There's no date on the note to tie it to that particular Friday."

"True. But if we learn he's part of your repressed memory, we might prove he was there."

"If I have a repressed memory," she reminded him. "I still have doubts about that."

"Why would Doug want to murder Carla?"

Deborah lifted a shoulder. "He may not have murdered her. Her fall still could've been an accident. I don't know of any motive he could've had for murder." A possibility occurred, and she snapped her fingers. "Wait a minute...was Carla pregnant?"

Milo shook his head. "That would've been in the autopsy report."

"Then wanting to avoid fatherhood wouldn't have been Doug's motive." Defeated, she sagged back against the sofa cushions.

Brows furrowed, Milo sipped his coffee. Then he set the mug on the coffee table and turned to Deborah. "What if we contacted Piper and persuaded her to tell us about the other lead she's working on? We'll offer to help her."

"But in her letter, she says she won't discuss it." Deborah picked up Piper's letter and pointed to the sentence.

Milo set his jaw. "I don't care. This is too serious for her to play games. Call her and tell her we're coming over."

"Now?" Surprise made her squeak out the question. Deborah looked at her wristwatch. Nearly nine o'clock.

"Yes, now."

Even in the short time she'd known Milo, Deborah recognized his "don't argue with me" tone. If she'd been strongly against making the call, she would've argued, anyway. But, this time, she and Milo were of one mind.

Deborah selected Piper's number on her cell phone. After half a dozen rings, she was switched to Piper's voice mail. "She's either not home or doesn't want to take calls. Shall I leave a message?"

"No. We're going over there."

Deborah turned to look at him. "But why? If she's not home…"

"We might catch her coming in. I have a strong feeling this can't wait."

Chapter Eleven

Fifteen minutes later, Deborah and Milo arrived at the Town Commons. Deborah gazed out the open window of Milo's car at the bright lights and throngs of people. Lively music came from the gazebo, where couples swirled around the dance floor, and the evening breeze carried the aromas of popcorn and barbecue. "This is the weekend of the Autumn Festival," she said. "The booths were being built the day I had lunch with Piper. Maybe she's at the festival tonight."

"Maybe." Milo slowed the car to take in the busy scene. "But we'll check her apartment before we try to find her in this crowd."

The other end of the Commons, where the Fairfield Arms sat, appeared deserted. Milo found a guest parking spot.

Soon they were inside the building. Looking around and seeing no one, Deborah hugged her arms. "This place feels creepy tonight."

"I agree. But I assume you want to walk up?" He pointed to the "Stairs" sign.

"If you don't mind."

The stairwell was empty. At Piper's fifth floor apartment, Milo grasped the gold-plated doorknocker. Before he could knock, the door swung open. He shot Deborah a raised-eyebrow look and then stuck his head inside. "Piper!" he called.

No answer.

Deborah leaned inside the apartment and called Piper's name, too, several times.

But no one answered.

"Do you think we should go in?" Deborah tensed.

"Yes, I do. This doesn't look good." Milo touched his foot to the door and edged it open.

Piper's brightly lit apartment provided a hopeful sign that she was there. Deborah and Milo went from room to room, calling Piper's name. In the kitchen, a pot of coffee sat on the coffee maker, the red On light shining. In her alcove office, the computer's screen saver, a montage of autumn leaves, floated back and forth on the screen. Books and papers were strewn across the desk.

Deborah read a few sentences on one of the papers. "This looks like her article on Burlington's population growth. She mentioned it the day we had lunch."

But no Piper.

Back in the living room, Deborah stood with hands on her hips, gazing around. "She has to be here somewhere—unless she went to the festival." Her gaze traveled to the balcony, and then she pointed. "Look, the balcony door's open."

"I didn't notice that when we came in." Milo headed toward the open door.

Deborah followed him and stepped out onto the patio's cement surface. A light breeze drifted from the dark woods across the way, along with the sounds of music from the festival. The balcony looked the same as it had the day Deborah was there for lunch—the metal chairs, the glass-top table, the potted plants.

Tonight, though, a stepladder had been added. The

ladder lay at an odd angle against the railing, as though it tipped over and came to rest there. Looking up, Deborah spotted a light fixture on the balcony's ceiling. "Was Piper changing the bulb?"

"Looks that way. The socket's empty, though, so she must have taken out the bad bulb."

"And something prevented her from putting in the new one. Maybe the new one is around somewhere." Deborah scanned the area. "You check that side of the balcony, and I'll check this side."

"Here it is," Milo said a few moments later. He pointed to a light bulb lying near the door. "Don't pick it up," he cautioned Deborah. "We don't know what happened here yet. Keep looking. We'll see what else we can find."

Deborah finished searching her side of the balcony and approached the railing. She gazed first at the woods across the way and then at driveway below.

Her jaw dropped and she stared, unable to believe her eyes. Blood pounded in her ears. "Oh, no!" she cried when she found her voice. "Milo, come quick!"

Milo rushed to her side. "What is it?"

Deborah pointed to a body lying in the driveway. Darkness shadowed the form, but she knew instinctively the person was Piper. She lay on her stomach, with her arms outstretched. Something dark had stained the pavement next to her head. Blood?

Time rolled back to four years ago, and Deborah stood in the gazebo at Rainbow Falls, looking down on Carla lying on the flat rock below. Dread pooled in her stomach.

"Call nine-one-one. I'll go down and see if she's alive."

Still lost in the past, she barely heard Milo's command.

"Deborah!" Milo grabbed her shoulders. "Get a grip and make the call."

Deborah blinked and pushed away the images flooding her mind. "Yes, of course. You go see if...if she's still alive."

Milo ran back into the apartment and out the front door.

Deborah pulled her cell phone from her purse. Her hands shook, but she managed to make the call and give Piper's address to the operator. Slipping her phone back into her purse, she peered over the balcony's railing.

Milo knelt beside Piper's body.

"Milo! Is she—"

He looked up, his expression grim. "I can't find a pulse."

Deborah's heart sank. She'd prayed Piper would be alive.

"You called for help?" he asked.

"Yes, they're coming."

"Good. I'll stay here. There's broken glass here, too. Looks like a light bulb." He pointed to a scattering of glass near Piper's body.

In the distance, sirens wailed, and soon the medics' van swung into the alley. The police arrived, led by Officer Noble, who appeared no older than twenty-five but whose no-nonsense manner and commanding tone left no doubt about his authority. Officer Noble followed Deborah and Milo out to the balcony.

Milo pointed to the tipped-over ladder and then to the bulb. "We think she might have been changing the light bulb, fell off the ladder, and then over the balcony.

I saw a broken bulb in the alley next to her body."

Officer Noble nodded and wrote in his notebook. "We'll check it out."

After answering all the officer's questions, Milo and Deborah were allowed to leave. They returned to her house, where Deborah made a fresh pot of coffee.

"I can hardly believe what happened tonight," she said when they were seated at the kitchen table.

Milo nodded, his expression grim. "Finding Piper in the alley was a shock, all right."

"Do you really think her death was an accident? I have this funny feeling…" She shuddered and wrapped her hands about the warm mug.

"Me, too."

"What if someone murdered Piper and made it look like an accident? Couldn't someone have pushed her over the balcony and then arranged the ladder and bulb to make it appear as though she were changing a bulb?"

"I suppose that's possible."

What she'd just suggested was awful and made her blood run cold. Deborah stood and paced from the table to the sink and back again. "If her death is connected to my visit and to the letter she wrote me, then I feel responsible."

"Now, Deborah," Milo warned. "Don't jump to conclusions."

"I can't help it." Tears burned her eyes. "I should have left well enough alone. I never should have probed into her affairs."

Milo came to her side and drew her close. "Deborah, stop it. You're not responsible. Don't punish yourself." He brushed a tear from her cheek.

Deborah slipped her arms around Milo's waist.

"But poor Piper. She had her whole life ahead of her. She had her career."

"Yes, her career. Maybe her death had to do with something she was investigating."

"I don't know what she was working on, other than the Burlington population article, or what she was doing regarding Carla." She nestled against his chest. "Do you think we should tell the police about the letter Piper sent me?"

"No, we'll wait and see what happens. We can always come forward later with our information, if we think that would be best. In the meantime, we'll continue our own investigation." He tipped up her chin. "What do you say? Are you still with me?"

Deborah gazed into his eyes "Yes, I'm in too far now to turn back."

"Thank you, Deborah." He touched her lips in a gentle kiss.

She sighed and laid a hand on his cheek. He smelled of soap and leather, and a maleness all his own.

"I don't want to leave you alone," he whispered, tracing the line of her lower lip with his forefinger. "Let me stay the night."

Let me stay the night. Images of the two of them lying in her bed upstairs flashed through her mind. If only things were different... Deborah shook her head. "That's not a good idea."

"I'm not suggesting we sleep together, although I must admit I wouldn't turn down the offer."

His teasing tone brought a smile to her lips. Still, letting him stay posed too big a risk. "I appreciate your offer, but I have to say no."

Milo let a beat go by and then breathed a heavy

sigh. "All right. But I'm concerned about your safety. If Piper was murdered, there's a murderer running around loose. Until he—or she—is caught, I'll worry about you."

Until the murderer is caught. She sucked in a breath and held it. What would happen after that? Would he still worry about her then?

****

A few minutes later, Milo drove along the road leading to Castletown—and home. Home was usually a place he enjoyed. But tonight, the image of his empty farmhouse brought an ache to his chest. The taste of Deborah lingered on his lips, as well as the memory of her sweet, subtle scent. Although he would have stayed the night, he knew her refusal was for the best.

But what he'd said about being concerned for her safety was entirely true. He was worried, and he would have been content to sleep on the sofa—even the old one in her parlor. Okay, maybe content wasn't the best word, but he would have managed.

Yes, he was concerned about her, but other, confusing emotions ricocheted through him. Sometimes, the long-buried anger and disgust made him never want to see her again. And sometimes the desire, such as he'd felt tonight, made him want to hold her tight and never let go.

The anger was toward the teacher responsible for Carla's death, the teacher who for four years had been without features or personality. Did he still feel anger toward the woman he now knew as Deborah Kent? Weren't she and the faceless teacher one and the same? Unable to sort out his feelings, he drove on, staring into the dark night.

****

The following day, Detective Sergeant Jurgens came to see Deborah. Older than Officer Noble, he had a weathered face and a jaded attitude. She led him to the parlor, where he perched on the edge of the sofa as though he didn't plan to stay long enough to get comfortable. His questions appeared to follow an established routine in which he had little personal interest. She told him the same story she and Milo had told Officer Noble. "What do you think happened to Piper?" she asked when he finished his questions.

Sergeant Jurgens shut his black notebook and tucked his pen into his jacket's breast pocket. "We don't know. The results of the autopsy haven't come back, for one thing."

"But could her death have been an accident?"

"Couldn't say."

After Deborah showed the detective to the door, she returned to the parlor. She grabbed a dust cloth from the closet and dusted the furniture, more to have something to do than because the room needed cleaning. She couldn't stop thinking about Piper and her horrible death.

Then Lacey phoned. "I just heard on this morning's news that Piper McCaffrey is dead!"

Clutching her dust rag, Deborah sank onto the sofa. "I know. Isn't it terrible?"

"Yes, I can hardly believe it."

"Milo and I found her." Deborah pressed a hand to her suddenly queasy stomach.

Silence filled the other end of the line.

Deborah raised her voice. "Did you hear me, Lacey?"

"Yes, I heard you. I'm just stunned. You and Milo found her?"

"We did." Deborah struggled with her emotions as she sketched in the details.

"That must have been awful," Lacey said.

"Seeing Piper lying in the alley was like being at Rainbow Falls and looking down on Carla's body. I felt the same horror."

"I'm sorry you had to go through that again. Is there anything I can do?"

"No, thanks, Lacey. I'll be all right." Deborah recalled that Piper had been a favorite pupil of Jay's. "How is Jay taking Piper's death?"

"He doesn't know yet. He's at a headmasters' convention in Boston. I called, but he's not answering his room phone or his cell. I left a message for him to call me."

"He'll be upset." Deborah swiped her cloth over a couple spots on the coffee table.

"I'm sure he will. He was fond of her." Lacey gave a sigh. "I'll be anxious to hear the official verdict of what happened. But her death certainly sounds accidental. What do you think?"

Still unable to overcome her sadness, Deborah slowly shook her head. "I don't know. I just don't know."

"You don't think someone killed Piper, do you? Why would anyone want to harm her?"

"I don't know," Deborah said again. "We'll just have to wait and see what the police decide."

****

Several days later, a police spokesperson announced that Piper's death had been ruled accidental.

Deborah and Milo attended Piper's memorial service held at the Janson Funeral Home. At first, Deborah did not want to go, but in the end she decided she needed to say a final good-bye to Piper.

At the service, Deborah and Milo signed the guest book and then followed an usher down the chapel aisle. As Deborah settled into her seat, she noticed Piper's parents sitting in the front row. She had met them four years ago at Wainwright's Parents' Night and found them to be a pleasant couple.

Sitting with the McCaffreys were a young couple and two small children, a girl and a boy. The woman's shoulder-length hair was the same chestnut shade as Piper's, and Deborah guessed she was a sister.

She also spotted Doug Jaspers, and a few rows behind him, Lacey and Jay.

After the service, Deborah and Milo attended the reception. They offered their condolences to Mr. and Mrs. McCaffrey, who introduced the young woman with the chestnut hair as Piper's older sister, Lisa.

"I remember you," Lisa said to Deborah. "You were the teacher involved with Carla Cassidy's accident."

Even though Lisa's tone was factual rather than judgmental, her words sent the familiar pain coursing through Deborah. "Yes, I was. And Milo is Carla's brother."

Lisa extended her hand to Milo. "You've lost a sister, too."

Milo nodded as he clasped Lisa's hand. "I know how sad you must be feeling right now."

"I'm so sorry about Piper," Deborah said. "We had renewed our acquaintance, and I was looking forward to our being friends."

Lisa gave Deborah a sad smile. "Piper would have made a good friend. She was extremely loyal."

Piper's parents stepped away to talk to other people, but Lisa remained with Milo and Deborah. They reminisced a bit about Piper.

Then, after a pause in the conversation, Milo cleared his throat and said, "Lisa, Piper was helping Deborah and me with an investigation."

Lisa raised her eyebrows. "She was? What kind of investigation?"

"We can't go into the details here, but if we could get together—"

Lisa's green-eyed gaze shifted back and forth from Milo to Deborah. "Well…all right. I am curious. I'll be at Piper's apartment next Wednesday, sorting her belongings. A job I don't look forward to, but one that has to be done. Why don't you come about one o'clock?"

Milo looked at Deborah, and when she nodded, he turned back to Lisa. "Thanks, Lisa. We'll see you then."

Chapter Twelve

The following Wednesday, Deborah worked on her house projects. But from noon on, she waited with tensed muscles for Milo to pick her up. She had been thinking about their appointment with Lisa, wondering if she and Milo would learn anything from the young woman.

Milo arrived at twelve-thirty on the dot.

Deborah stood at the front door, watching him climb from his car and head up the walk. The sight of him never failed to stir her senses. Today he looked as handsome as always, dressed in jeans, a navy blue sweater, and a gray windbreaker.

As he bounded up the steps, he looked up, caught her gaze, and grinned. "Hi. Ready to go?"

"Yes, I've been waiting. Just let me grab my purse and jacket."

"Should we have a plan for how we'll approach Lisa?" Deborah asked when she sat beside him in his car and they were underway. "Should we tell her Piper believed Carla was to meet Doug Jaspers at Rainbow Falls the day of the accident?"

Milo slowed the car at the end of the cul-de-sac to let another car pass by. "We'll play it by ear. She seems trustworthy, but we don't know that for sure. I doubt she'd agree her sister might have withheld information about Carla's death."

"I think you're right. We'll know more what to do when we talk to her." Deborah settled back and gazed out the window.

Fifteen minutes later, Lisa admitted Deborah and Milo to Piper's apartment.

"We appreciate your seeing us today," Milo said as he stepped inside.

"We won't stay long," Deborah added.

Lisa closed the door and then rubbed her red-rimmed eyes with the back of her hand. "That's okay. I need a break. I've been sorting Piper's clothes. I plan to give them to her favorite charity."

"I'm sure your donations will be appreciated," Deborah said.

"I'm the only one in the family who can cope with this," Lisa said over her shoulder as she led them along the hallway. "Mother, especially, can't bear to come here, and so she's taking care of the kids."

While passing through the dining room, Deborah scanned the area, her gaze falling on the table where she and Piper had eaten lunch, and her chest tightened. On that day, she and Piper were about to change their relationship from student and teacher to peers and, hopefully, to friends. Now, Piper was gone, and Deborah would never have the opportunity to know her as either.

In the living room, Lisa moved a pile of sweaters from the sofa to the glass-top coffee table and motioned for Deborah and Milo to sit. "So, what's this investigation Piper was doing for you?" She slipped into a chair across from them.

Milo leaned forward and clasped his hands. "Lisa, were you satisfied with the verdict that your sister's death was accidental?"

Lisa frowned. "Why do you ask?"

"Because Deborah and I have some doubts."

Lisa's troubled gaze moved from Milo to Deborah.

"That's true, Lisa." Knowing how upsetting their news might be, Deborah kept her tone gentle.

Lisa folded her arms. "At first, I had some doubts, too. I thought Piper might be investigating something dangerous. But when I arrived today, the first thing I did was step onto the balcony and walk through what was supposed to have happened. I understood how the investigators reached their conclusion."

"Could you walk through that again?" Milo asked. "Maybe that would help us to understand, too."

Lisa bit her lip. "I don't know...How my poor sister died is not something I want to dwell on."

"Me, either." Deborah scooted forward in her seat. "And I'm sure Milo feels the same way. But, Lisa, making sure Piper's death was truly an accident is important."

"Well...all right. But after that, I'll expect you to tell me what this is all about."

When she first stepped onto the balcony, Deborah kept her gaze straight ahead, but like a magnet, the driveway captured her attention. She walked to the railing and gazed down. The dark spot she'd seen near Piper's body still remained. Her stomach knotted. Had Piper suffered? Or been killed instantly? What terror had she experienced during those fleeting moments between the beginning and the end of the fall?

Milo joined her and slipped his arm around her waist. "Take it easy, Deborah. I know this is tough, but the process might help us."

Comforted by his gesture and reassuring words, she took a deep breath and let the tension in her stomach uncoil. "Thanks, Milo. I'll be okay." Deborah turned and gazed around the balcony. "Everything looks the same as that night, except the ladder is missing."

"It's in that storage closet." Lisa pointed to a door at one end of the balcony.

"Mind if I take out the ladder again?" Milo stepped toward the closet.

Lisa heaved a sigh. "No, go ahead."

A couple minutes later, Milo had the ladder positioned under the light fixture. "We'll see how an accident could have happened." He placed a foot on the ladder's bottom step.

"Be careful." Deborah raised a cautioning hand.

He tossed her a grim look over his shoulder. "I will, don't worry."

At the top, he stretched an arm toward the fixture. "Okay, I'm removing the bulb. Then on the way down, I suddenly lose my balance, and the ladder tips toward the balcony." He descended and tipped the ladder to one side. The ladder came to rest on the balcony's railing.

"Yes, the accident could have happened that way." He turned to Lisa. "What about the broken bulb I saw in the alley?"

"That bulb was burned out. And the one you spotted on the floor here was a good one." Lisa pointed to a spot on the balcony floor.

Milo rubbed his chin. "So, she removed the bad bulb, intending to descend the ladder with it, exchange it for the good one, and climb back up."

"She probably didn't want to juggle two bulbs at once." Deborah gazed up at the empty light socket. "But why was she changing the bulb herself? Why didn't she ask the maintenance person to do it?"

Lisa came to stand beside Deborah. "I was here a few days before she fell. It was evening, and we sat here for a while. I remember the bulb was burned out then. I mentioned it, and Piper said since she had a ladder she would change the bulb herself, rather than call maintenance."

No one said anything for a few moments, and then Milo broke the silence. "So far, everything points to an accidental death."

"Yes." A sinking sensation invaded Deborah's stomach. She'd hoped they would discover something to indicate the opposite.

"I still want to hear what you promised to tell me." Lisa gestured to the door. "Come back inside, and we'll talk."

When once again they all were seated in the living room, Milo began, "First of all, like we told you earlier, Deborah and I have reason to believe my sister Carla's death was not an accident."

Lisa widened her eyes. "You mean someone might have killed her? But at the inquest, her death was ruled accidental."

"True." Deborah nodded. "But as Milo said, we have reason to believe otherwise."

"What reason?" Lisa sat forward and propped her chin on her fist.

Milo shot Deborah a warning look and then turned back to Lisa. "We can't tell you right now."

"You don't think Piper was involved, do you?"

124

Lisa's voice rose. "She was Carla's best friend."

Milo spread his hands. "No, we don't think your sister was involved. But information she gave Deborah raised questions about the accident."

"What information?"

"Again, we can't tell you. We need to keep that confidential until we have everything figured out."

"Piper had more information she planned to give us." Deborah tensed, hoping Lisa couldn't detect that she stretched the truth. "But we never got it."

"So you think Carla might have been murdered." Lisa clutched the arms of her chair. "And you think Piper was murdered, too? Don't you?"

"We don't know for sure about either of them." Milo kept his voice calm. "We're only speculating."

"What you're implying can't be true." Lisa's eyes glistened with tears. "We've just shown how her death was an accident."

"I'm sorry." Deborah stood and patted Lisa's shoulder. "We don't mean to upset you. But you said earlier you had misgivings, too."

Lisa sighed. "All right, yes. I did have a hard time accepting her death as accidental. I never liked the idea of her being an investigative reporter. I always wanted her to do something safe. I wanted her to find a nice guy, get married, and raise kids, so we could all be one big family."

She shook her head. "But, no, she had to have a career investigating. Anyway, I couldn't help but think she might have dug up something someone didn't want her to write about. But I never thought her probing might be connected to Carla's accident."

"Will you let us take a look at Piper's office and

what she was working on?" Milo asked.

Lisa narrowed her eyes. "I don't know. Maybe you're out to frame Piper for Carla's death. Then you wouldn't have to bear the responsibility anymore, would you, Deborah?"

Deborah winced inwardly, but she kept her voice firm. "We want to find out the truth. Don't you believe the truth is important?"

Lisa folded her arms and stared at the floor.

Deborah caught Milo's glance.

He pressed his lips together and shrugged.

Finally, Lisa looked up and nodded. "Okay, you can examine her office." In Piper's alcove office, Lisa stood to one side and watched while Milo searched the two-drawer file cabinet, and Deborah riffled through the papers on the desk and in the drawers.

After a few minutes, Milo closed a file drawer and turned. "Nothing of interest." He looked at Deborah. "Did you find anything?"

Deborah held up a flash drive.

"Mind if we check the computer?" he asked Lisa.

Lisa shrugged. "Go ahead." She told him Piper's password.

Milo turned on the machine and scanned the hard disc's contents. "Nothing here." He held out his hand. "I'll try the flash drive."

Deborah handed him the drive and stepped behind his chair.

He plugged in the device and accessed the information. After a few minutes, he sat back and shook his head. "Just a backup of what's on the hard drive."

"Did Piper keep her work anywhere else?" Deborah turned to look at Lisa. "Maybe she didn't want to leave sensitive material lying around for someone to see."

"I don't know of any other place." Lisa absently straightened a stack of papers on the desk. "But I haven't gone through everything in the apartment, either."

Milo shut off the computer and returned the flash drive to the desk drawer. "If you find anything you think might be of interest to us, will you let us know?"

Lisa sighed. "All right. But I think you're making a big mistake to dig up the past. You should leave well enough alone."

****

Later, when Milo turned into Deborah's cul-de-sac, he pointed to a blue sedan on the way out. "That car looks familiar."

Deborah glimpsed a young, red-haired man behind the wheel. She pressed her lips together and shook her head. "Albert Healy paying me a visit again. He certainly doesn't discourage easily."

"He'd better not have tampered with anything."

Milo's grim tone left no doubt about his feelings toward the troublesome young man. "I set the alarm system before we left." Deborah hoped her attention to security would reassure Milo.

After parking his car, he walked around the yard, poking at the bushes, and then insisted on coming in and inspecting the house from top to bottom.

When Milo was satisfied no intruder had been in the house, he sat in the kitchen and drank a cup of fresh-brewed coffee.

They made small talk, but Deborah sensed something else was on his mind. Seeing his cup was empty, she rose and retrieved the coffee pot. "Would you like a refill?"

"No thanks." He took the pot from her hand and set it on the table. Then he drew her down onto his lap. He put his arms around her, cradling her against him in a warm hug. "Deborah…" he murmured, and then tipped up her chin and covered her mouth with his.

She returned his kiss, savoring the sweetness of his lips, the thrill of being in his arms again. When the kiss was over, not wanting to be apart just yet, she sighed and laid her cheek against his chest.

They sat for long moments, neither speaking, yet volumes passing between them. After a while, he raised her chin with his forefinger and gave her another, passionate kiss that filled her with warmth and desire.

"Let me make love to you, Deborah," Milo whispered. "We'd be good together."

Deborah yearned to give in and make love with Milo. But that would not change their situation. She was still the teacher responsible for his sister's tragic death. And afterward, he would probably resent and perhaps even hate her. She shook her head. "No, Milo."

Grasping her shoulders, he gazed into her eyes. "No, what? No, you don't want to?"

"That's not the reason," she said in a quiet voice.

"What, then?"

"You ought to know. Carla. She'll always between us. No matter what we find out about the accident, nothing will change the fact I didn't supervise the girls as closely as I should have." She squeezed her eyes shut against the painful memories.

Milo lowered his gaze and remained silent.

"I'm right, aren't I?" Her insides shook, but she

had to hear his answer.

Still, Milo said nothing.

Yet, what had she expected? Did she want him to lie and say, no, Carla was not between them? Of course not.

Her wandering gaze landed on the coffee pot, bringing her back to the present. She pulled away and placed her palm against the pot's glass side. "The coffee's cold now," she announced. "But I can warm it up, if you want."

Milo released her and shook his head. "I'd better be on my way."

"Milo…please don't think I didn't like what we were doing just now…"

He laid a hand on her shoulder. "I know you enjoyed the kisses as much as I did. And, don't worry, okay? Everything will work out."

But would it? Deborah stood at the front door, once again watching him drive away.

Chapter Thirteen

For the next few days, Deborah could almost believe her life had returned to normal. She received no notes and saw no one sneaking around her property. Could the harassment be over? If so, had Piper been the culprit? Deborah did not want to believe Piper was her stalker. That the harassment ended at the same time Piper died must be coincidental.

On Saturday, a little over a week after the visit to Piper's apartment, Deborah had scheduled her second appointment with Dr. Lawton. Despite her doubts, she had decided to continue the sessions. Deborah debated whether to remind Milo of her appointment or to say nothing and make the trip alone. Since the awkward scene after their visit with Piper's sister, he had called a few times, but their conversations were brief and limited to discussing Piper's death. Neither had learned anything new to report.

"I won't be able to go with you to see Bob," he said when he phoned on Tuesday. "I have to deliver a mare to a guy in Chesterton. I wanted to arrange another time, but he insisted I come on Saturday."

"That's all right." Although disappointed, Deborah kept her tone light.

"I'm really sorry, I wanted to be with you for all your appointments. Will you be all right alone?"

Deborah straightened her shoulders. "Of course, I

will. I've been taking care of myself for quite a few years now."

"I know you have, but not under these dangerous circumstances."

"Nothing has happened for over a week."

"Your stalker might be hoping to catch you with your guard down. That worries me. Promise me you'll be careful."

"I will."

On the drive to Burlington, Deborah missed Milo even more than she thought she would. The thirty miles, which sped by when they traveled them together, today seemed like sixty. Not even listening to the radio helped to pass the time.

The glowing colors of the countryside were fading, reminding Deborah winter was not far off. She dreaded the thought of gray skies and ice and snow, and wished autumn would last forever.

Upon arrival in Burlington, she found a parking place on the street and soon entered the revolving doors of the Cobb Building. Since today was Saturday, no one was around. Her footsteps echoed through the high-ceilinged lobby. She climbed the stairs as fast as she could. Again, she wished Milo were with her. Perhaps she should have changed today's appointment to a time when he could have come, too.

In Dr. Lawton's office, the receptionist greeted Deborah, and after a short wait, he appeared and ushered her into his cozy office. As before, she sat on the sofa in front of the gas fireplace. She kept her spine rigid and twisted her hands in her lap. What if today she finally recovered her lost moments? What would happen then?

Dr. Lawton soon guided Deborah into a trance. Once again, he used the mental staircase to help her access the past.

She shifted in her seat, struggling to concentrate. Finally, she reached the bottom of the stairs. Once there, she solidly rooted herself at the falls, where she relived the event with more clarity and detail than she had the last time she was under Dr. Lawton's guidance.

Still, when she reached the part just before she tripped and fell, she came up against the usual mental blank wall.

"Linger there awhile," Dr. Lawton instructed. "Remember, nothing can hurt you. You're only an observer. What do you see? What do you hear?"

Hearing the doctor's calm voice, Deborah concentrated on being an observer. She saw herself running down the path in her attempt to reach Carla. The landscape flew by, trees and underbrush and ground blurring like watercolors running together on a painter's palette. A bright object caught Deborah's eye. "I see something," she said aloud.

"What is it?"

"I don't know, but it's round and shiny."

"Where is this round and shiny object?"

Deborah squeezed her eyes tighter shut and concentrated. "In the trees."

"Hanging in the trees?"

"No…oh, the sunshine hit it. It's glowing now."

"Are you sure you don't know what it is?"

Deborah focused on the bright object. Nausea pushed up from her stomach into her throat. "No! No! I don't know what it is!"

"Walk away, Deborah," Dr. Lawton said in a

soothing voice. "Walk away."

"I-I—" Tears streamed down Deborah's face and dripped onto her hands lying in her lap. Her breath came in short gasps.

"Take a deep breath. Then turn your back on what you see and return to the staircase."

Deborah managed to follow Dr. Lawton's instructions. When she opened her eyes, she saw him leaning forward in his leather chair, a tissue in his outstretched hand. "Thanks." She took the tissue and scrubbed her face. Then she leaned back and closed her eyes. After a while, Deborah raised her head and offered Dr. Lawton a weak smile.

"I think you had a breakthrough." He picked up his clipboard and pen and made a few notes. "Do you have any idea now what the shiny object might be?"

"No." Deborah rubbed her forehead. "And thinking about it hurts my head."

"Then don't. Forget about it, and wait to see if your unconscious pushes anything to the surface."

Deborah twisted the tissue in her hands. "I don't know if I want the object to surface. I feel so…threatened."

He gave her a reassuring smile. "Remember you're an observer, and whatever happened then cannot hurt you now."

Deborah wasn't so sure. However, her "breakthrough," as the doctor called it, encouraged her, and before leaving the office, she made another appointment.

Still shaken by what she'd experienced, she more loathe than ever to use the elevator and headed directly for the red neon Exit sign and the stairs. She opened the heavy steel door and entered the stairwell. The door closed behind her with a loud clank. On her last visit, she had not noticed the cold atmosphere or the ugly green walls. Today, the stairwell resembled a prison. Eager to escape, Deborah hurried down, her flat-heeled shoes clattering on the cement steps.

On the floor above, a door opened and slammed shut. She expected to hear footsteps echoing either up or down, but all was silent. Perhaps the person had only peeked into the stairwell and then decided not to use the exit. Nervous and jumpy, Deborah stepped up her pace. She reached the third floor and rounded the landing to the second, when behind her, the door to the third floor opened with a whoosh and a blast of cold air.

Before she could glance over her shoulder to see who had joined her, she felt someone wrap an arm around the neck. Her body stiffened, and her breath caught in her throat. The assailant jerked Deborah's head back against his chest. She had the sensation of bulky clothing and something rough covering the person's face. A ski mask?

The person tightened the chokehold, and her windpipe closed. Deborah gasped for air. She flailed her arms, but he captured her right wrist and twisted her arm behind her. Spots danced before her eyes. She groped with her left hand for something to hang on to and grabbed the iron stair railing.

At the same time, she bent her leg and aimed a backward kick. Her heel connected with something solid, like a shin. A muffled oath sounded close to her ear.

Her effort threw her assailant off balance, but not enough to make him release her neck. Pressure to her windpipe increased, and blackness curled around the edges of her vision. Just when Deborah knew she would die if she couldn't gulp in some air, she felt the arm around her throat loosen and then drop away. She gulped in a much-needed breath, and her vision cleared. A sharp thrust, like that of a knee, hit the middle of her back. Her feet flew out from under her, and she tumbled down the stairs. Her screams bounced off the walls and echoed throughout the stairwell.

Each contact with the hard cement created a stab of pain. She hit the bottom, slid across the landing, and slammed into the opposite wall. Stars whirled before her eyes. Vaguely, she was conscious of footsteps climbing above her, of the opening and shutting of a door. Then silence.

Gradually, her vision cleared, and she sat upright, propping her back against the wall. Her neck and throat burned. Her left wrist throbbed, and warm blood trickled down her cheek. She must get out of the stairwell. Her assailant might return. Looking around, she spotted her shoulder purse lying nearby. Why hadn't her attacker taken it? Wasn't that what he—or she—was after? But why the chokehold? Why not just grab the purse and run?

Deborah struggled to her feet, but a wave of dizziness made her plant a hand flat on the wall. With great effort, she picked up her purse. Leaning over brought more dizziness. She propped herself against the wall until the sensation passed and then with shaking fingers looped the purse strap over her shoulder.

Gripping the iron railing and taking each step in slow motion, Deborah made her way down the remaining flight of stairs to the lobby. When she pressed her hands against the cool metal of the Exit door handle, she felt a sharp pain in her left wrist.

Should she go to the nearest ER and have her injuries assessed? No, she didn't want to fill out forms and answer questions. Neither did she want to return to Dr. Lawton's office—afraid of meeting her assailant on the way. She wanted to be on her way home as soon as possible.

What if her sore wrist hindered her driving? Better have someone come and get her. The first possibility was Milo, but he was out of town. What about Lacey? What were best friends for if not to rescue each other in times of need? If Lacey was available, she would be more than willing to drive to Burlington and pick her up. Deborah fished in her purse for her cell phone and then withdrew her hand. No, she would not call Lacey, or anyone else. She would take care of herself.

A man rounded the corner of the hallway. Fearing he might be her attacker, Deborah tensed, ready to run. Then she noticed he wore the blue uniform and cap of a security guard. Still, she must be careful. A uniform was no guarantee this man was not her attacker. A lined face and white hair peeking out from under his cap put him in his fifties.

When he saw Deborah, he drew his brows together in a frown. "Are you all right, miss?"

Deborah pushed back a lock of hair and smoothed her jacket. She smiled and lifted her chin. "Yes, I'm fine."

"But your cheek looks like it's bleeding."

Deborah pressed her hand to her cheek. Her fingers came away wet with blood. "I fell in the stairwell."

He hurried to her side and gripped her elbow. "You

fell? Then come with me and fill out an accident form."

Deborah jerked away. "No!" Then she took a deep breath and said in a calmer voice, "I mean, no, thank you. I'm all right. You don't need to report anything."

The man's eyes darkened. "You fell on the property. We need to make a report."

Deborah pulled a tissue from her purse and patted her cheek. "No. I have to leave now." She backed away, toward the revolving front door.

"Management don't like accidents to go unreported. They worry about law suits."

"I won't sue. Falling down was my own fault. I lost my footing."

"You have to come with me," the man insisted. "I need to do my job." He reached for her arm again.

Deborah whirled and ran, which wasn't easy as pain spiraled through her left leg. Still, she was out the revolving door before the security man could catch up. A glance over her shoulder showed him standing on the top step with feet planted apart, hands propped on his hips, and a scowl twisting his face.

But he didn't follow her.

Despite her throbbing wrist, Deborah drove with caution. Along the way, she couldn't keep her thoughts from whirling. Was the attack random? Or planned? Who could have known exactly when she would be in the stairwell?

Reaching the Fairfield city limits eased her tension. Yet the thought of returning to her empty house left her cold. More than anything, she wanted to see Milo and tell him what had happened.

Instead of taking the route to her house, she headed for his. If he weren't there yet, she would wait. Not wanting to miss the turnoff, she leaned forward and peered through the windshield. At last, the road appeared ahead. She turned and, a few minutes later, spotted the roof of his house peeking through the trees. The thought of being with Milo again calmed her jangling nerves. He would know what to do.

A few minutes later, Deborah staggered up the porch steps and rang the doorbell. Leaning against the doorjamb, she waited. She expected Katie to appear, but no one came. Deborah limped along the driveway to the back of the house. She passed the pond, where the ducks glided, and then the garden, with its cheerful nest of flowers.

Her gaze fell on the stable. Perhaps one of Milo's employees could tell her when he'd be home. But only the horses were there. She heard them softly nicker and stopped to pat the nose of one as she passed by its stall.

Sick with disappointment, she returned to her car, climbed in, and curled up on the front seat. Her next awareness was of someone gently shaking her shoulder and calling, "Deborah! Deborah!"

She opened her eyes and raised her head. "Milo?" Was he really here at last? Or was she only dreaming she saw his handsome face?

"Yes, it's me. What are you doing here? Your cheek looks like it's been bleeding. What happened? Never mind now. We'll get you inside."

Relief washed over her. "Of course, I knew you were out of town. But I thought Katie would be here."

Milo put his arm around her waist and kept her close as he helped her from the car. "Katie's visiting relatives in Castletown."

Inside the house, he led her down the hall to a

black-and-white tiled bathroom where he settled her on a padded stool. "We'll get the cut on your cheek fixed first."

Milo opened the medicine cabinet and took out a plastic bottle of disinfectant. He wet a washcloth, gently wiped the scrape, and then applied the medicine with a cotton swab.

Stinging attacked her cheek, and Deborah flinched. "Ouch!"

"Sorry. But I need to make sure the cut doesn't get infected."

"I know." She settled herself more securely on the stool. "But I didn't come here for you to doctor me."

Milo taped a gauze bandage over the wound. "Then why did you come?"

"I-I'm not sure. But after what happened, I didn't want to go home to an empty house."

"I'm glad you came. I'm only sorry you had to wait so long. I'm late getting back because I drove by your house on the way home."

She pressed a hand to her chest. "You were coming to see me?"

"Yes. I wanted to hear about your appointment with Bob." He laid a hand on her shoulder. "When I saw you weren't home yet, I thought you'd stopped to do errands. I called your cell and left a message. I waited awhile then came home."

Her pulse kicked up a notch. "I turned off my phone during the session with Dr. Lawton and never turned it on again. But thanks for your concern."

"Of course, I'm concerned." He gazed into her eyes and brushed a lock of hair from her forehead. "Now, do you have any other injuries?"

Forcing a movement against the dull throbbing, she held up her left arm. "My wrist. And my leg." She pointed to her left leg.

Milo gently probed her wrist. "I don't think any bones are broken, but the only way to be sure is to have it X-rayed. I can take you to the ER."

Deborah flexed her wrist. "No, I don't want a doctor. Although the injury hurts, I'm sure it's a sprain, at the most."

Milo frowned. "Okay, I'll go along with you...against my better judgment, though. But if the pain worsens, we're off to the hospital."

"I promise I'll let you know. How about my leg?" Bracing her hands beneath her thigh, Deborah stretched out her left leg.

He knelt and examined the bruises. "I have some ointment to put on these. And then I'll wrap your wrist." After opening a cupboard, he took out a glass container of ointment and a beige cloth bandage.

She watched him, shaking her head in wonder "Where'd you learn to be such an expert at doctoring?"

"In the army. Comes in handy, once in a while. Like now." He shot her a grin. When he finished tending her bruises and wrapping her wrist, Milo helped Deborah to the kitchen and sat her at the round table. He made a pot of spice tea, and soon the fragrance filled the room. They sipped the brew in silence for a few minutes, and then Milo put down his cup. "Now tell me what happened."

She began with her visit to Dr. Lawton and finished with, "Do you think the attack was random, or was someone after me, specifically?"

Milo sat back and folded his arms. "A mugger

could have panicked and not taken your purse, but my gut feeling says the person was after you. Someone could have followed you to Bob's office and waited until you came out. Then he—or she—saw you head for the stairs and followed."

A chill swept over Deborah, and she hugged her arms. "That gives me the creeps."

"Someone may have tampered with your car, someone did send you threatening notes, and stalked you at home. So why couldn't they attack you in the stairwell, too?"

"You've got a point. But whoever's responsible gets bolder. This was an assault on my person."

"That's what worries me." Milo picked up the teapot and refilled their cups. "Maybe your attacker was Doug Jaspers. He's afraid Piper told you about the note he wrote to Carla, and now you think he's involved in Piper's death."

Deborah nodded and sipped her tea. "Or the person could be Damon Healy, or his son, Albert."

"Albert." Milo snapped his fingers. "Hearing his name reminds me of something I found. I'll be back in a minute." He jumped up and strode from the kitchen. A few minutes later, he returned carrying a slim book with a green padded cover and laid it on the table. "This is the high school yearbook for the year Carla died."

Deborah ran her fingers over the embossed letters that spelled out "Fairfield High School" and then looked up at Milo. "Where did you get this?"

Milo slipped back into his chair. "I wanted to know more about Doug, so I went to the high school. I told a friendly receptionist I was Carla's brother. She remembered the accident. I said I wanted to look up some of Carla's friends and asked if she had a yearbook I could see. She found the book and ended up giving it to me."

"That was nice of her."

"I thought so. Anyway, I found Doug's picture in several places, but also someone else of interest." He opened the book and flipped through the pages. Placing his finger on one of the portraits, he turned the book in Deborah's direction.

Deborah studied the photo of a young man with red hair and a long, thin face. "Albert Healy." The name below the picture proved she was correct.

"Yes. He was in Doug's class." Milo turned more pages. "Here's a picture of Albert as the geology teacher's assistant." He showed Deborah a photo of Albert and several other students. The caption read, "Teaching Assistants Toe the Mark."

"I remember Piper said the class Doug might have skipped was geology," Deborah said.

"Right. Plus, Albert and Doug were both on the baseball team, and I'm betting they were buddies." He tapped the page with a forefinger. "Albert could be responsible for the attacks, not only to get you to sell your property but to protect Doug Jaspers as well."

"The deeper we dig, the more possibilities we come up with," Deborah mused.

Milo chuckled. "Like peeling the onion."

They discussed Albert and Doug, and then Deborah's session with Dr. Lawton. During a lull in the conversation, Deborah glanced at the wall clock and saw the time was nearly five o'clock. "I'd better go home." She scooted to the edge of her chair.

"I don't think so." Milo's tone was firm.

"What?" Deborah raised her eyebrows. "I need to go. I just wanted to talk to you for a while and tell you what happened."

He leaned forward and took her hand. "I'll look after you tonight. You've had a very rough time."

Deborah's shoulders tensed. "But—"

"You don't need to worry. I won't take advantage of you, certainly not while you're injured and in pain. Even though I might like to."

Milo's eyes sparkled with teasing. Still, Deborah remained rigid. "But I…where—?"

"Where will you sleep? I have a guestroom. Plus, Katie left spaghetti, French bread, and a salad for dinner. All I have to do is heat it up."

Hearing the offer of a guestroom, Deborah grinned and leaned back in her chair. "How can I refuse such a deal?"

"Hmmm, I notice that when I offered dinner, you finally agreed." He turned down his mouth. "I hoped my company compelled you to stay."

"Dreamer." She grinned.

Milo put the pot of spaghetti on the stove, and soon the aroma of meatballs and tomato sauce filled the air.

Deborah offered to help, but he insisted she relax. So, she looked on while he set the table, brought out the salad, and popped the French bread into the oven. The food was delicious, and Deborah relished every bite.

Afterward, Milo built a fire in the living room fireplace. They sat on the sofa, basking in the glow of crackling flames. He put his arm around Deborah, and she laid her head on his shoulder. They watched a couple of TV sitcoms, laughing at the actors' antics.

Presently, Milo looked at his wristwatch. "Ten

o'clock. I'm ready to call it a night. How about you?"

"Yes, I'm ready."

As she watched him turn off the TV and extinguish the lights, Deborah felt her nerves tighten. Would he change his mind about letting her sleep alone in the guestroom and persuade her to join him in his bed?

They climbed the stairs, with Milo supporting her so she could keep weight off her injured leg. Halfway down the hall, he stopped and opened the door to a bedroom. Deborah held her breath, but then exhaled when she saw the room's lack of personal items, which confirmed it was the promised guestroom.

He pointed out extra pillows and blankets in the closet, towels and toothbrush in the adjoining bath. Then he snapped his fingers. "I just thought of something. Wait here."

She sank onto the bed, pulling up her sore leg, and waited, wondering what else she could possibly need.

A few minutes later, he returned, carrying an oversized T-shirt. "Will this do for a nightgown?"

She stared at the shirt. "Ah, sure. That will be fine."

He laid the shirt on the bed and then leaned down and grasped her shoulders. "Okay, time to say goodnight."

She expected him to kiss her lips, but his lips landed instead on her forehead in a feather-light, chaste kiss.

"Sleep well," he whispered, and was gone.

Deborah sat there, shaking her head. She truly didn't understand herself. She had feared he might make advances, but now that he hadn't, disappointment filled her. Her gaze fell on his T-shirt. Did she really want something of his as sleepwear? Maybe she should sleep in her underwear. She lifted the shirt to her face. The cloth was full of his masculine scent. With a sigh, she peeled off her clothes and pulled the shirt over her head.

****

Milo laid awake, watching shafts of moonlight glide across the hardwood floor of his bedroom. Having Deborah spend the night proved more difficult than he'd thought. Only a wall separated them. He wanted with all his heart and soul to hold her in his arms and make love to her. Would there ever be a time for them?

A sound awoke him. He bolted upright. What was that? He heard it again—a woman's cry.

Deborah.

Leaping out of bed, he grabbed his jeans and pulled them on. He ran from the room, down the short stretch of hallway that separated their rooms, and burst into hers.

Deborah was sitting up in bed, clutching the sheet to her chest.

He hurried to her. "Deborah, what is it? Are you in pain?"

Moonlight shining through the cracks in the blinds showed her face wet with tears and her eyes filled with terror. He sat beside her and laid a hand on her trembling shoulder. "What happened?"

She gave him a blank look.

Alarm coursed through Milo. What was wrong with her? He rubbed her shoulder reassuringly. "It's me, Milo. I heard you cry out."

"Milo? Oh…Milo."

Seeing recognition soften her frightened eyes, he

sucked in a relieved breath.

"I-I had a nightmare. The one about Carla...where...where I'm trying to reach her at the bottom of the falls. Oh, it was so awful." She pressed a hand to her forehead.

"There, there," he soothed. Putting both arms around her, he drew her close. Her skin felt feverish and damp, and her hair was in tangles. He smoothed back her hair and wiped the tears from her cheeks. "It's okay. It was only a dream."

"A dream? But so real. So...so horrible."

"I know. I understand. But the dream is over now. In a little while you'll be calm enough to go back to sleep."

She heaved a deep sigh and snuggled into the crook of his arm. He continued to hold her and stroke her back. After a while, he whispered, "Think you're ready to sleep again?"

"I...I guess so."

"Here, get under the covers." He shifted so she could wiggle down into the bed. He caught a glimpse of long, slim legs, and the curve of her bottom, where the T-shirt didn't reach. His pulse spiked. He sucked in a breath and pulled the sheet and the quilt over her. "Okay now?"

"Yes, but I'm afraid to fall asleep. Sometimes I have more than one nightmare."

"Should I stay awhile?"

She gripped the quilt and gazed up at him. "Could you?"

"Of course. Can you move over a little?"

She scooted to the right, and he slid under the covers. Turning on her side, she curled up with her back against his chest. He put his arm around her and breathed in the fragrance of her hair.

"Thank you, Milo," she murmured and then sighed, deep and long.

Soon her even breathing told him she was asleep, but he lay awake, his thoughts churning. Who had attacked her? And why?

Chapter Fourteen

The following Monday, back at home, Deborah maneuvered the vacuum cleaner over the parlor carpet with her right hand, while holding the cord lightly in her left. Her wrist still ached, and so did her leg, but she was determined to keep on task.

The doorbell sounded over the roar of the vacuum.

Oh no, she hoped the caller wasn't Albert Healy. If so, she wouldn't answer the door. She shut off the machine and peeked out the window. When she saw Lacey standing on the porch, she breathed a sigh of relief and hurried to open the door.

"Thank God, you're all right." Lacey rushed inside and threw her arms around Deborah.

As she embraced Lacey, Deborah caught a whiff of alcohol, once again raising her concern for her friend. Still uneasy with discussing the subject, she said nothing.

Lacey drew away and looked into Deborah's eyes. "I've been so worried about you. I called you several times Saturday night and again on Sunday, but you didn't answer." Her gaze roved Deborah's face. "Heavens, what happened to your cheek? And your arm's in a bandage. Were you in an accident? Tell me."

"I'll tell you over a cup of tea." Actually, Deborah needed time to think. Should she tell Lacey the complete truth about what happened in Burlington, or not? She wanted to, because she always shared confidences with her good friend. But Milo wanted to keep their investigation to themselves.

Lacey looked at her wristwatch. "I have a meeting of the museum board in half an hour, but I have time for a quick cup."

"Good. Let me take your coat."

Lacey shrugged out of her brown wool jacket.

Deborah hung it in the foyer closet.

In the kitchen, Lacey insisted on retrieving the cups from the cupboard while Deborah put the teakettle on the stove and set out the tea bags and sugar and creamer.

At last, they were seated at the kitchen table with their tea.

Lacey drummed her fingers on the table. "Now, tell me what happened."

Deciding to give Lacey only selected information, Deborah began. "When I was leaving Dr. Lawton's office building on Saturday, I fell in the stairway. You know I avoid elevators when possible."

Lacey nodded and stirred her tea. Some of the brew sloshed over the brim of the cup and onto the saucer. "But you weren't home last evening. Did you go to a hospital?"

"No. I went to Milo."

"And you were with him all night? Are you two having an affair?" Lacey leaned forward, her gaze intent.

Deborah's cheeks heated at the memory of sharing a bed with Milo, so chastely, yet so intimately, too. "No, but what if we were? We're both adults."

"But he's Carla's brother." Lacey's brows drew

into a frown.

Deborah looked away. "There's not much we can do about that, is there?"

Lacey asked a few more questions, which Deborah deftly fielded. After a while, Lacey looked at her watch. "I've got to run."

As Deborah led Lacey to the front door, she heard the doorbell ring. "Better not be Albert," she muttered, detouring to the window to peek out. Not Albert this time, either, but the mailman. She opened the door.

"This was too big to put in the box." He handed her a large manila envelope and then turned to leave.

When Deborah saw the sender was Lisa Marshall, she felt her heart beat faster. Had Piper's sister found something among Piper's belongings she thought Deborah and Milo would be interested in?

Lacey peered over Deborah's shoulder. "What's that?"

"Ah, I don't know. I'll open it later." She pressed the envelope to her chest, hoping Lacey had not seen Lisa's name. Then guilt nudged her. Why was she keeping secrets from her best friend?

Lacey smiled. "I'm glad you're all right. Let me know if anything comes up that I can help you with. I want the best for you. You know that."

"Thanks." She handed Lacey her coat. "I will let you know. I want the best for you, too, and I expect you to tell me if you need my help."

"I will," Lacey promised.

When she was alone again, Deborah took the envelope into the parlor and sat on the sofa. Still thinking about Lacey, she wasn't ready to open it yet. The house was quiet now that her friend was gone.

Today a tornado of nervous energy surrounded Lacey. Something wasn't right.

Perhaps she and Jay were having a mid-life crisis. If that's the case, she hoped they worked out their problems. She would hate to see them split up after they had achieved so much together. Finally, Deborah opened the envelope. Inside were six printed sheets of paper, stapled together. A note attached to them said:

"Deborah and Milo,

I found these in Piper's safety deposit box at her bank. I have no idea whether or not they will help you, but since the papers concern Carla, I am passing them along.

Lisa Marshall"

Deborah turned to the stapled papers. In the upper left-hand corner of the first sheet were Carla's name, "U.S. History," and a date that corresponded with Carla's attendance at Wainwright. The papers appeared to be an assignment for Jay's history class, in the form of a newspaper article. The headline read, "Boys Murder Stepbrother," and the dateline was Chicago. The text related a chilling story about two twelve-year-old friends named Dean Standifer and Peter DeWitt. Dean decided to murder his new stepbrother, ten-year-old Bobby Martin.

Peter helped Dean carry out his plan by leading Bobby to a cabin in the woods where Dean waited. Dean stabbed Bobby to death. Dean was arrested and charged with murder. Peter was held as an accessory to the crime. The article did not tell what happened to the boys.

On the last page was a handwritten note:
"Carla,

This does not fulfill the assignment, which was to write a newspaper article based on an important event in history. Please drop by my office, and I will help you pick a suitable topic.

Mr. Grant"

Deborah scanned the papers again, and a chill washed over her. Why would Carla write about such a horrible incident? And why had Piper secured the article in her safety deposit box? The assignment must have great importance if it had to be hidden away. She wished Piper had made a note about the significance of the article, but the packet Lisa sent contained nothing else.

She put down the papers and picked up the phone to call Milo. Two heads might be better than one for figuring out the meaning.

Fortunately, Milo was available to come directly to her house.

She had a fresh pot of coffee waiting when he arrived. He took a moment to give her a hug, which she eagerly returned. Any sign of affection reassured her that he did care, even a little. In the kitchen, she handed him a mug of coffee and the papers Lisa sent. "See what you make of this."

Milo read, not taking away his gaze when he sipped his coffee. When he finished, he looked up. "What a strange story."

"Yes, and so evil. Twelve-year-old kids plotting to kill another kid. Just thinking about it gives me the chills." She hugged her arms.

"I would agree with Jay's comment that this hardly fulfills the assignment." He rubbed the back of his neck. "Why would my sister write something like this?"

She shrugged. "I can't imagine. And how did Piper get it? And why did she keep it in her safety deposit box?"

"So many unanswered questions." Milo tapped the papers with his forefinger. "But suppose this incident really happened?"

Deborah put down her cup and gave Milo her full attention. "Okay, suppose it did. Then what?"

"Then we need to know why she chose it for this particular assignment."

"We may never determine that."

"I know, but this is the only lead we have. We'll follow it as best we can. First, we need to know if this story is true. The Internet ought to help us."

"Right. Let's go to my office." In Deborah's office, they sat together at her computer. After accessing a list of sources, she chose an article from a Chicago newspaper. "This looks like what we want."

After he read the selection, Milo leaned back in his chair. "So, the murder Carla wrote about really took place."

"Yes, the names are the same and so are the details. In fact, Carla's close following of this article makes me think she must have read it. But why she thought it would fulfill the assignment is a mystery."

They perused several related articles. One followed up the initial story by stating Dean Standifer was found guilty of murder. He was sentenced to a juvenile correctional facility until age twenty-one. As an accessory to the crime, Peter DeWitt went to the same facility for four years.

Another article, dated ten years later, said Dean Standifer died in an adult prison where he was serving time for armed robbery. He was stabbed to death in a fight with another inmate. How ironic that Dean would die by the same method he used to murder his stepbrother.

"I wonder what happened to Peter DeWitt," Milo said.

Deborah sent the articles to the printer. "Maybe we could hire a private detective to find out."

He patted her shoulder. "Good idea."

"We still don't know why Carla used this story to fulfill her assignment for Jay's class."

Milo shrugged. "Maybe she wanted to do something different from what the other kids were doing."

Deborah picked up Carla's assignment and idly fingered the first sheet. "We could ask Jay. He might give us some insight into why Carla wrote about such a horrible tragedy."

"Uh uh." Milo shook his head. "Like I said before, we need to keep what we discover to ourselves."

Deborah added the articles they'd printed to the one Carla wrote and squared her shoulders. "But I'm sure Jay wasn't involved in your sister's death. I would trust him with my life. He's one of the finest, truest men I have ever known."

"Maybe so, but I don't want to talk to him just yet. First, I want to follow your suggestion and hire a PI to locate DeWitt."

A few minutes later, they stood at the front door, saying goodnight. Milo slipped his arm around Deborah's waist. "Did I tell you how pretty you look today?"

His husky tone set her heart fluttering. "No, you

didn't. But in jeans and a sweatshirt?" She gestured at her outfit.

"You look pretty in anything." He caressed her cheek. "Even though I might be preoccupied with our problem, that doesn't mean I haven't noticed."

She gave him a warm smile. "Well, thank you for telling me just now." She expected him to pull away and leave.

Instead he lingered, keeping his arm around her waist.

Finally, he spoke, his voice low. "I wish we'd met under different circumstances."

Ah, so that's what was on his mind. Her smile faded. "I wish we had, too."

"But we didn't, and nothing can ever change what happened at Rainbow Falls, can it?"

Sadness washed over her. "No, nothing can change that."

He was right. And because of the tragedy, she and Milo had no future together. No future at all.

Chapter Fifteen

Deborah tacked the last piece of yellow brocade onto the arm of the chair and then stepped back to view her work. Her wrist had finally healed enough to resume her upholstering, and she had spent the past few days recovering two chairs purchased at a garage sale.

She was making good progress on the house, but much remained to be done before she could open her bed-and-breakfast. As she placed the last tool in the toolbox, she heard the doorbell ring. Who could her visitor be?

Deborah hurried to the door, hoping her visitor was Milo. Several days had passed since she had heard from him, and she longed for the sight of his handsome face, the sound of his deep voice. Whenever they parted, she worried they might not ever see each other again. Her insecurity—and her guilt over the past—kept her on edge.

Two men stood on the doorstep—Damon Healy and a man she did not recognize.

"We need to talk to you, Deborah," Damon said.

"Mr. Healy," Deborah began in a firm voice, "I've told you and Albert, too, that I do not want to sell my house."

A sly smile crossed Damon's face. "I think you'll change your mind when I introduce you to Hank Dobson." He gestured to the other man.

Deborah dropped her jaw. "Hank Dobson!"

"Yes, this is Rose's long-lost husband."

Pulse racing, Deborah stared at the stranger. "I thought you were—"

"Dead?" Hank Dobson snorted. "Nope. Alive and well."

"Now, then," Damon said, "don't you think you'd better let us come inside and have that talk?"

"All right." Deborah opened the door wider to admit the men. In the parlor, she motioned for them to sit.

Damon chose the sofa and Hank a wing chair.

She considered offering them coffee, but quickly dismissed the idea. As uninvited guests—no, as intruders—she owed them no courtesies. She slipped into a chair across from the two men. What a contrast they were. Although overweight, Damon was immaculately groomed and distinguished-looking in his gray suit and black dress shoes. Hank was short and skinny in jeans and a brown parka with a ragged sheepskin collar. A vinyl cap with sheepskin flaps dangled from one hand.

Hank gazed around. "So this is the house Rosie bought with my money. Damon tells me you're fixin' to open a B-and-B."

"That's right." She turned to Damon. "What do you want to see me about?"

Damon cleared his throat. "I'll come right to the point. Hank and Rose never got divorced. Were you aware of that fact?"

Deborah shifted in her chair. "Rose told me he ran off. How could she divorce him if she didn't know where he was?"

"After he'd been gone seven years, she could have divorced him in absentia. But she didn't."

"She thought he was dead." Deborah struggled to keep her voice even.

"But she never checked to make sure, did she?"

Deborah spread her hands. "Why, I don't know. I never asked her."

"Well, now he's returned to Fairfield and wants to settle here."

"Let me see if I can guess the rest of this scenario." Deborah narrowed her eyes. "Mr. Dobson wants to claim this property so he can sell it to you." She focused on Hank. "Isn't that right, Mr. Dobson?"

Hank jutted out his pointed chin. "I haven't made up my mind. I might want to live here myself."

"But the house belongs to me." Deborah pressed a hand to her chest. "Rose left it to me in her will."

"The property wasn't hers to leave," Damon said. "Not all of it, anyway. Since they were never divorced, half of the house belongs to him. He can contest her will and claim his share." He nodded in Hank's direction. "So, unless you're prepared to buy him out…"

"Buy him out?" Deborah gripped the arms of the chair. "I could never offer him as much as I'm sure you already have."

"I'm prepared to make you both a generous offer." Damon named a sum.

Deborah gasped at the amount. "I don't want your money. I'll never give up what's rightfully mine—be it half the house or all of it—without a fight. You can both count on that. And now if you'll excuse me, I'm very busy." Pulse racing, she jumped up. Hands on her hips, she glared at the two men. She wanted them out of her house. She couldn't stand their presence a minute longer.

Damon and Hank exchanged glances.

Deborah couldn't tell what, if any, message passed between them.

Damon looked up at Deborah and opened his mouth.

"No." She held up her hand. "I don't want to discuss this any further."

"I hope you don't regret your decision, Deborah," Damon said, as he slowly rose to his feet. "A legal fight will be costly."

"You'll have to prove this man is who he says he is."

Damon smiled. "That's the least of our worries. Hank has solid identification."

She shifted her gaze to Hank.

He stood, too, and glowered from under bushy eyebrows.

A chill rippled over her skin.

"We'll be in touch," Damon said as he went out the front door.

"I like what you're doin' to the place," Hank said before following Damon.

Deborah shut the door on her unwelcome visitors and then took a deep breath. She needed a lawyer to help her cope with this latest development. The only lawyer she knew in town was Stanley Kaslow, who'd handled Rose Dobson's estate. She returned to the parlor, picked up her cell phone, and accessed his number.

Moments later, he came on the line.

As calmly as she could, she explained the situation. "Does this Hank person have any claim on my property?"

"First, as you pointed out to Damon, the man will have to prove he is Hank Dobson," Stanley said. "If he is, then his claim might very well carry weight."

A sinking feeling invaded Deborah's stomach. "That wasn't what I wanted to hear."

"I know. What a mess. When I drafted Rose's will, I had no idea she might have a husband alive somewhere whom she never divorced."

Deborah paced the room. "I guess she believed he was dead, or even if alive, he'd never return. Rose wasn't one to take care of legal matters. I'm lucky she left a will at all."

"Yes. Well, I'll get right on this. If either Hank or Damon contacts you again, refer him to me. You don't have to put up with their harassment."

"Thank you, Stanley. I really appreciate your taking over."

Stanley laughed. "That's what lawyers are for."

After Deborah ended the call, she went to work sewing curtains for the north bedroom. Although Stanley's reassurance eased her distress, she couldn't get her recent visitors out of her mind. So Hank Dobson wasn't dead, after all. She wondered where he'd been living all these years and exactly when he'd returned to Fairfield.

A chilling thought crossed her mind. Maybe Hank Dobson was the one who'd been harassing her. Armed with knowledge of her involvement in Carla's death, he could've tampered with her car and written the threatening notes. He could've dressed in black and come in the yard that night. And, yes, he could've followed her to Burlington and attacked her in the stairwell. He was harassing her so she would sell to Damon Healy. When none of his ploys worked, he came out in the open with a legal claim.

But now that she still refused, what would he do? Would he attack her again?

She picked up the phone to call Milo and tell him this latest development. "I think our stalker has come out of hiding," she said when he answered her call. She related her visit from Damon Healy and the man who claimed to be Hank Dobson.

"Your reasoning certainly sounds possible," he said, "but we'd better not jump to conclusions. I am glad you called, though, because I have some news, too."

Deborah gripped the phone. "Something from your PI?"

"Yes, but I'd rather tell you in person than over the phone."

"I'll be here the rest of the day, if you want to come over."

"See you in half an hour, tops."

****

Twenty minutes later, Deborah led Milo into the parlor. "I can't imagine what your news is that you couldn't tell me over the phone."

Milo sat on the sofa and patted the seat beside him. "Sit, and I'll tell you." He pulled a legal size envelope from the inside pocket of his jacket, removed several sheets, and handed them to Deborah. "This is an article the PI found, which wasn't on the Internet."

Deborah took the papers and read aloud the

article's headline. "'Teens Convicted in Murder of Stepbrother.' Okay, so what's different about this article?"

"Photos we haven't seen are included. Look on the second page."

Deborah slid aside the first page to reveal three portraits, one of each of the boys involved. Dean Standifer, the boy who committed the murder, had blond hair, cold eyes, and an arrogant tilt to his chin. The victim, Dean's stepbrother, Bobby Martin, appeared younger than his ten years. He was a cute kid with a cowlick, freckles sprinkled across his nose, and a mischievous grin.

The third picture was that of Peter DeWitt, who led young Bobby to the cabin where Dean attacked and murdered him. Deborah stared at the picture of the brown-haired youth, who had a hint of a smile and intelligent eyes. Something about him struck a familiar chord. The seconds ticked by and recognition finally dawned.

Deborah's heartbeat raced. The article slid from her hands and landed on the floor. "Peter DeWitt is Jay Grant," she whispered. "I can't believe it."

"Neither could I." Milo bent to retrieve the article. "But my guy confirmed his identity."

Deborah wrapped her arms around her waist and leaned forward. Knowing Jay's role in the terrible crime sickened her. "So now what do we do?"

"We talk to Jay." Milo lifted his chin.

"But what if he is involved with Carla's death, after all?"

Milo pounded a fist into his palm. "Then all the more reason to talk. We'll go to Wainwright and confront him there. He won't dare try anything in a public place. If he's not involved, then maybe he can shed some light on this matter."

"When shall we go?" She agreed with Milo's decision, but dread filled her at the thought of a confrontation with the man she considered her friend.

Milo stood and planted his feet in a wide stance. "The sooner the better."

****

They left in Milo's car and half an hour later reached the Wainwright Academy. The sight of the familiar brick buildings brought a lump to Deborah's throat. She had not been on the campus for four years, and here she was today, on a strange, and possibly dangerous, mission. What would happen when they confronted Jay with their knowledge of his past?

Milo parked in the visitor's parking lot. Deborah heard the clock on the tower strike two o'clock as she accompanied Milo across campus to the main building.

A group of girls sat on the building's steps, enjoying the last of autumn's warm days. They stopped chatting to cast sidelong glances at Deborah and Milo.

At the door, Deborah ground to a halt. Her heart thudded, and her palms felt clammy. Did she really want to go in? What if someone recognized her? The students wouldn't, of course, for they were all different from when she taught there. But surely some of the teachers and the clerical staff were the same. Would they speak to her? Or would they regard her with horror and disgust?

Milo gripped Deborah's elbow. "This is hard for you. I can talk to Jay alone while you wait in the car."

Deborah took a deep breath and lifted her chin.

"No, I'll be fine. I want to go with you. I haven't come this far to back down now."

They entered the building and walked down the marble-floored hallway filled with students heading for their next class.

"There's Jay's office." Deborah pointed to the door where a sign read, "Headmaster."

When Deborah saw that Jay's secretary was not the same woman who had worked for Dr. Hammer, she gave an inward sigh of relief.

"May I help you?" the woman asked.

Milo approached her desk. "I'm Milo Jordan, and this is Deborah Kent. We're here to see Dr. Grant."

The woman slipped on a pair of gold-framed half glasses and consulted her computer screen. "But you don't have an appointment."

"No, we don't." Deborah stepped up beside Milo. "But we must see him. Just tell him Milo and Deborah are here."

"We'll make an appointment," the secretary said in a firm tone. "I believe he has free time tomorrow afternoon."

The door to Jay's private office opened, and he stepped out. "Oh, Lori," he began, and then stopped. "Well, this is a surprise."

"We need to talk to you, Jay," Deborah said.

He widened his eyes. "Now?"

"I told them they need an appointment." Lori waved a hand.

"This can't wait, Jay." Milo folded his arms.

Jay wrinkled his brow, gazing first at Milo and then at Deborah. Finally, he nodded. "Okay. Come on in my office." He turned to his secretary. "Hold all my calls, will you, Lori?"

Being in Jay's office reminded Deborah of the times she'd been there to see Dr. Hammer. On the first occasion, she was a newly hired teacher. The last was the day he told her she was dismissed. She pushed away the memories and concentrated on today's visit.

Jay seated Deborah and Milo and then eased into his high-backed leather chair behind his desk. He leaned forward and studied them. "Now, what's troubling you two?"

"We need to talk to you about Carla's death," Milo said.

Jay pressed his lips together. "I had a feeling that was your purpose. I heard you two were drumming up a different scenario than the official one. Have you succeeded?" He leaned back and folded his arms.

"I'm not sure we've 'drummed up another scenario,'" Deborah said, twisting her fingers together, "but we did uncover something disturbing."

"And what's that?"

"Piper's sister, Lisa, gave Milo and me an assignment Carla wrote for your history class." Deborah pulled out Carla's essay from an envelope in her purse and slid it across Jay's desk.

Jay put on a pair of reading glasses and perused the article. His eyelids flickered but when he looked up, his expression betrayed no emotion. He tossed the papers onto the desk. "I wonder why Piper had this?"

"That's what we want to know," Milo said. "We thought maybe Carla had written about a real crime, so we did some research."

Jay smirked. "My, my, you are determined, aren't you? Does being responsible for Carla's death bother you that much, Deborah?"

The barb stung. Rudeness was so unlike Jay, but perhaps being on the defensive had unleashed another side of his personality. A potentially dangerous side. Inwardly, Deborah shivered. Maybe confronting Jay was a mistake, no matter how public the place. "We found out Carla wrote about a real murder." She handed the rest of the papers from her envelope to Jay.

He perused them with the same unrevealing expression as before. Then he took off his glasses and leaned back in his chair. "This is all very interesting, but I don't see the point—"

Shaking his head, Milo raised a hand. "Come on, Jay, quit playing games. Look at the picture of Peter DeWitt. That's you."

Instead of looking at the picture, Jay swiveled to gaze out the window behind him. Several moments of tense silence passed.

Deborah clutched the arms of her chair and looked at Milo. His raised eyebrows said, "Wait awhile longer."

Finally, in a barely audible voice, Jay spoke. "Yes, I am, or was, Peter DeWitt."

Hearing him admit the truth made Deborah's mouth go dry. No, not Jay. Not her friend and fellow-teacher.

Jay turned his chair to face them again. "So, what do you think of me now?"

"We'll reserve judgment until you tell us your side of the story." Milo shrugged.

Jay heaved a deep sigh. "All right. But not here. We'll go for a walk on campus."

Chapter Sixteen

In the outer room, Jay told Lori he was taking Deborah and Milo on a tour of the campus. Then he led them down the long, now-empty hallway toward double doors leading outside. Before he reached the doors, Jay stopped in front of a glass display case. "Look at all the trophies." He pointed to the rows of silver and gold statuettes, cups, and bowls. "Last year we won the regional debate tournament for private schools. Two years ago, our basketball team came in second in the state playoffs."

Pride ringing in his voice, he pointed out other awards.

Deborah stepped closer and read some of the engravings. "All these have occurred since you've been headmaster."

"Yes. In fact, this trophy case wasn't even in existence during Dr. Hammer's time. I bought it."

They continued through the double doors to a courtyard filled with wrought-iron tables and chairs.

"This area is new, too," Deborah remarked as she glanced around.

Jay nodded. "The student council voted to create it. We've had several fundraisers. And see the gym?" He pointed toward the square building on the other side of the courtyard. "Remember, Deborah, how the roof leaked? A new roof was the first major upgrade under my leadership."

They walked around the gym, where a large section of land had been cleared and a foundation dug. A chain link fence kept the area protected from trespassers.

Jay stopped and rested a hand on the fence. "This is our most ambitious project to date. Can you guess what it's to be?"

"A theater?" Milo tapped his foot.

"Not just a theater, but a performing arts center. With an arts center, we'll attract many talented students and give them the very best opportunity to develop their skills."

"You've done a lot since you've been headmaster." Although Deborah admired Jay's accomplishments, she wished he would move on.

"I want you to keep all this in mind when you hear my story." Jay gave them a solemn look. He led them back to the courtyard and waved them into chairs. "I was an abused child," he began, "but I'm not using that as an excuse for what I did. I'm telling you because that's part of my history."

"Abused by both parents?" Deborah flinched at the thought.

Jay shook his head. "Just by my father. He beat both my mother and me. My mother escaped into alcohol. Her drinking finally killed her when her liver failed. But that was a long time later, and after my father had passed away, too.

"Anyway, I was a pretty mixed-up kid. I trusted few people, but once someone was decent to me, I would do anything for them. That's why I took up with Dean Standifer." Jay stared at the ground. "He befriended me, he treated me okay, and I started palling around with him. I knew he had a mean streak, but so what? I was used to that.

"When Dean's divorced father remarried and Bobby Martin became his stepbrother, Dean freaked out. He didn't want another kid competing for his father's attention. He almost ran away from home." Jay frowned and rubbed his forehead. "He should have. Then our lives would have turned out differently."

Jay's obvious distress in divulging his troubled past brought an ache to Deborah's throat.

"In truth, Bobby was a brat," he continued. "He tormented Dean, like putting mice in his bed. But what really pushed Dean over the edge was when Bobby took Dean's beautiful golden retriever out in the woods and let him loose. The dog never came home. Dean was heartbroken. He vowed he would teach Bobby a lesson. He asked me to help set a trap for Bobby, so he could give him a good licking.

"So, I did. I led Bobby to the cabin where Dean waited, just like the newspaper article said. I never dreamed Dean would kill Bobby, and that's the honest truth." He looked first at Milo and then at Deborah.

The anguish in his eyes told her he spoke the truth. "I believe you."

Milo nodded, his expression grave.

"After I delivered Bobby, I took off. I didn't want to hear him screaming when Dean beat him. That would remind me too much of my own experience. You know what happened after that. Bobby died. We got caught, tried, convicted, and sent to a juvenile prison."

"Being imprisoned must have been an awful experience." Milo shifted in his seat.

"It was. But, amazingly enough, something good

came from the ordeal. A counselor I met there made me realize that even though I was responsible for what I'd done, I could still make something of myself. When I was released, I was a changed person. Sadly, Dean wasn't. He got into trouble again, and you know what eventually happened."

Being reminded of Dean's fate made Deborah's heart ache. With the same opportunity Jay had, he, too, might have been rehabilitated.

"But, even though I decided to do something useful with my life, I thought I would have a better chance as someone else, not as Peter DeWitt. So, I changed my name to Jay Grant. I went to college, studied to become a teacher, met and married Lacey, and here I am." He made a sweeping gesture to include the campus.

"Does Lacey know about your past?" Concern for her friend tightened Deborah's stomach.

Jay waved a hand. "Yes, she knows. She's always been very supportive. I'm lucky to have her as my wife."

Milo frowned and folded his arms. "So where does Carla enter in?"

"Yes, now we come to Carla." Jay slowly shook his head. "Stupidly, I kept all those newspaper articles at home, in a desk drawer. Carla babysat for us, and one night when the boys were looking for something in the drawer, they pulled out the articles."

"So your sons know about you, too." Deborah winced.

"No, they don't. They never read the articles. But Carla did." Jay pursed his lips and shook his head. "And then she tried to blackmail me."

"No!" Milo jumped up. "She wouldn't do

something like that. Not Carla."

Shock rippled through Deborah. Would Carla really do such an awful thing? And if so, Milo would be devastated.

"I'm sorry, Milo," Jay said. "I know you loved your sister. But she did threaten blackmail. She wanted desperately to get out of Wainwright, but your mother and stepfather insisted she attend. You know that, don't you?"

Milo sank back into his chair. His shoulders slumped and his mouth turned down. "Yes, that's true."

"She did everything she could to get expelled, including sloughing off on her schoolwork. But Dr. Hammer, not wanting to upset the Cassidys, still wouldn't expel her. I didn't know she knew my secret until she turned in that assignment." He raised his eyebrows. "I have to admit, she was clever."

"A note from you was on the last page, asking her to meet with you." Deborah's mind raced.

"Yes, and we did meet. She made it clear she would expose me unless I somehow convinced Dr. Hammer to expel her. I tried to reason with her, telling her I didn't have that kind of influence with Hammer. But she wouldn't listen. She gave me an ultimatum of two weeks."

Milo clasped his hands together and stared at the ground. "This is so hard to believe." He looked up at Jay. "But go on. What happened then?"

"Rainbow Falls happened." Jay's voice dropped a notch.

For several seconds, no one spoke. Deborah risked a glance at Milo. His ashen face tore at her insides.

"But I didn't kill her." Jay straightened and stuck

out his chin. "I know you're both still thinking maybe I did. At the time of her accident, I was at the doctor's office. If you don't believe me, you can check up on it."

"I believe you," Milo said in a choked voice. "I remember your alibi was part of the official report and was verified."

"I believe you, too." Deborah spoke the truth. Deep down, she knew Jay could never cause Carla's death. What had happened with Dean Standifer and Bobby Martin had taught Jay a hard lesson.

"Thanks." Jay gave her a sad smile and then turned to Milo. "I know this is hard, Milo, but Carla was a very mixed-up youngster. Don't think too harshly of her. I don't. I just wish I could have done something to help her."

"Me, too." Milo shook his head. "I had no idea she was so disturbed."

Inside the main building, a bell rang.

"That's the end of fifth period," Jay said. "I need to get back."

On the way to the entrance, Deborah fell into step beside Jay. "Did Lacey know about Carla's attempt to blackmail you?"

"No, I never told her. I didn't want to upset her. I was confident I'd convince Carla to drop her scheme. But I made a mistake by giving back the article she wrote. After her death, I wondered what became of it, but I didn't dare ask." He shrugged.

"When nothing happened to indicate anyone else saw the assignment, I assumed either Carla had destroyed it, or her parents had, not knowing its awful significance. Obviously, the paper wasn't destroyed and came into Piper's possession. I suppose we'll never know exactly how that happened."

"I wonder if Piper was on to you." Deborah mounted the steps to the door.

"I'm sure she wasn't. She probably hadn't had time for investigating Carla's article, if that's what she intended. I saw her shortly before her death, and her manner toward me was as warm and cordial as always."

They reached the building's entrance. Before opening the door, Jay stopped and, hands on his hips, turned, and surveyed the campus. "I've been happy here. My life has been useful and productive. Oh, I probably would be happier if I were still a teacher. My being headmaster was Lacey's idea, you know." He cast them a smile. "But that's neither here nor there. I am the headmaster, and I'm doing a good job."

"You are, Jay." Deborah laid a hand on his arm.

Jay narrowed his eyes. "So what will you two do with all this?"

Deborah held her breath as she looked at Milo. Would he expose Jay and bring about an end to his career? Or would he allow Jay to continue as Wainwright's headmaster?

Milo pressed his lips together and gazed off into the distance. Several tense moments passed. Then he turned back to Jay. "What will we do? I'd say, absolutely nothing. What about you, Deborah?"

Deborah expelled her breath. "Oh, Milo, I agree. We don't even want those articles or the report from the PI. Why don't you destroy them, Jay?"

"All right." Jay was silent a moment and then he added, "I truly believe Carla's death was an accident. I hope you two can come to grips with that and get on with your lives."

"I hope we can, too," Deborah said.

As Jay reached for the door, he stopped and snapped his fingers. "I just remembered something. We're having a party at our house on Saturday night for Lacey's and my twentieth wedding anniversary. Will you two come?"

Although still reeling from all he'd told them, Deborah wanted to support her long-time friend and colleague. "I'm free that evening."

Milo nodded, but his eyes were bleak.

Back at Milo's car, Deborah slipped into the passenger's seat and then laid a hand on Milo's arm. "I'm so sorry about what Jay revealed about your sister. Are you okay?"

He started the car and headed out of the parking lot. "Accepting that Carla tried to blackmail Jay is tough. She could have ruined his career, and all for her own selfish reasons."

"I know. But, please, like Jay said, don't be too hard on her. She was unhappy and mixed up."

"That doesn't excuse something like blackmail."

Milo had high standards. He couldn't forgive Deborah for her negligence, and he couldn't forgive Carla for her error in judgment. His stubbornness saddened Deborah, but she couldn't change him.

They reached her house, and Milo parked at the curb. "Would you like to come in?" Deborah asked. "I can fix us a light supper."

He shook his head. "I wouldn't be very good company right now. I need to be by myself for a while and work through this."

Deborah nodded, but her insides twisted with hurt and disappointment. She wished he would let her help him through this bad time.

"I'll see you Saturday," he said when he'd walked her to the door.

Watching him drive away, Deborah felt more alone than she had in a long time.

Chapter Seventeen

The following day, Deborah was comparing samples of wallpaper in the parlor when Milo phoned. She put down the samples and sat on the sofa, eager to talk.

"I can't escort you to the Grants' party," he said. "There's an important horse auction in Rockville I need to attend. I've had the event on my calendar for months, but I didn't remember it when Jay mentioned the party."

Deborah's shoulders sagged, but she kept her voice cheerful. "That's okay. I can go by myself."

"We might be out of touch for a while," he continued.

"Do you still need time alone to accept what we learned about Carla?"

"Yes. And I've been doing a lot of thinking…about us."

Her mouth dried and her stomach tightened. "I know what you're thinking, too, Milo. Even though Carla tried to blackmail Jay, her action doesn't change the fact I'm still responsible for her death."

Milo's silence confirmed Deborah's accusation.

"You can't forgive her for what she did, and you can't forgive me, either. Why don't you just come right out and say it?" she challenged.

"I suppose you're right. But neither can you

forgive yourself. So, we're both in the same bind, aren't we?"

"Good-bye, Milo." Deborah yanked the phone from her ear and ended the call. Tears welled up and streamed down her face. With all her heart, she wished she'd never come back to Fairfield, or met Milo Jordan.

****

On the morning of the Grants' anniversary party, Deborah looked out the window to find a layer of silver frost on the lawn and the trees. Winter was indeed around the corner. She spent the morning wallpapering the south bedroom, and then took a break to wrap the white porcelain clock she'd bought for Lacey and Jay's anniversary.

That afternoon, Lacey called. "I'm so glad you're coming to our party tonight. But I'm sorry Milo had to cancel."

The reminder of her last conversation with Milo set her stomach churning. "Me, too."

"I'm hearing distress in your voice. Is everything all right between you two?"

For the first time, Deborah realized she didn't want to confide in Lacey. And, of course, she couldn't discuss her and Milo's visit with Jay, not when Jay had never told Lacey about Carla's blackmail attempt. "Everything is fine." She forced a cheerful tone.

"The weather forecast is for freezing temperatures tonight. I hope the roads won't be too slick to drive."

"I'll manage," Deborah assured her. Later that afternoon, Deborah changed from work clothes into navy blue slacks and a fancy white silk blouse. In consideration of the weather, she chose a pair of sturdy flats, rather than high heels. She brushed her flaxen hair until it shone and highlighted her cheeks with blusher and her mouth with a bright red lipstick. She wanted to look cheerful, even if she didn't feel that way.

Outside, her skin tingled in the crisp night air. Overhead, a bright moon hung in a glossy black sky. She drove out of town, following the same route she and Milo took when they attended the Grants' dinner party. The thought of Milo brought a rush of sadness and longing. She wondered what he was doing at the horse auction. Would the event include social activities? People to have dinner with, to party with? She wished she were at his side. Wherever he was, she wanted to be, too.

At the Grants', the maid took Deborah's blue wool jacket and then showed her into the living room where at least thirty guests were gathered, including those who had been at her hosts' earlier dinner party. She spotted Damon Healy and his wife, Ester. Their son, Albert, and Doug Jaspers escorted two young women who were former Wainwright students. Deborah made sure she greeted all of them politely and with her head held high.

Lacey approached, martini glass in hand. "So glad you could come, Deborah."

Lacey looked lovely in white slacks and a rust-colored pullover sweater, but her smile appeared forced, and her voice held a false ring. Was something troubling her?

Jay, handsome in black slacks and a gray shirt, gave Deborah a hug. But he, too, appeared to be putting on a show, laughing loudly at a guest's corny joke and waving his glass of Scotch as he talked.

Recalling her discomfort at the Grants' previous party, Deborah hesitated to circulate among the guests, but as the evening wore on, she relaxed and mingling became easier. Even when she overheard someone mention her former teaching career and the accident, she didn't flinch. Deborah realized she had finally accepted the past. Yes, she had made a mistake, for which she had dearly paid. Even if she didn't receive Milo's forgiveness, she would forgive herself and carry on with her life. Feeling as though a weight had been lifted from her shoulders, Deborah smiled and concentrated on enjoying the party.

At eight o'clock, Jay and Lacey led everyone into the dining room for an elegant buffet supper, featuring prime rib, roasted potatoes, and an assortment of salads. Deborah filled her plate and found a seat at one of several card tables set up around the room. She introduced herself to her three seatmates, women who served with Lacey on the museum's board of directors. They made pleasant small talk while they ate.

Presently, Jay rose and tapped his coffee cup with his spoon. "May I have your attention, please?" Conversation ceased, and he continued, "I'd like to thank you all for helping Lacey and me celebrate our twenty years of marriage." He smiled down at Lacey, who looked up at him over the rim of her martini glass.

"I have a gift for Lacey. But first, I want to tell you a story about it. Lacey and I spent our honeymoon in France. In a Paris jewelry store, I saw something I wanted her to have. I hadn't bought her a wedding present yet, and I thought this would be perfect. Luckily, she liked my gift, too." He paused to acknowledge polite laughter rippling around the room.

Deborah was following Jay's story with interest when something flickered in the corner of her eye.

179

Something round and shiny. Startled, she jerked her head to look around but didn't see anything that could have been the object she'd glimpsed. Again, she turned to Jay, but had trouble focusing on his words. Something significant had happened a moment ago, but she wasn't sure what.

In a casual way, she let her gaze sweep the room. Some of the guests were standing so they could see Jay and Lacey better. Deborah's gaze passed over several, including Damon, Albert, and Doug. Damon had unbuttoned his suit jacket and stuffed his hands in his trousers' pockets. He turned to speak to his son, and his tie clasp caught the light from a nearby lamp.

Deborah stared at the large gold circle clipped to his dark brown tie. A locked door in her mind sprang open, and she remembered with stunning clarity a shiny gold circle reflected in the light from an autumn sun beaming down through the trees at Rainbow Falls. She gasped and pressed a hand to her chest. Had she seen Damon Healy on the path that fateful day? Was he connected to Carla's death?

Dr. Lawton said her lost memory, prompted by something familiar, might return at any time. Deborah blinked, hoping to expand the picture in her mind. Yes, she was sure she had seen someone wearing something round and shiny, but the person's features were hazy. Try as she might, she couldn't bring them into focus.

Damon swung his head in her direction and gave Deborah a fierce look that chilled her bones.

Danger hummed along the airwaves, surrounding Deborah, suffocating her. She had to escape. Now. Vaguely, she was aware Lacey was opening her anniversary present from Jay, but she could not wait even for that.

"Are you all right?" one of her tablemates whispered. "You look pale."

Deborah touched her stomach. "I'm a little queasy. I-I think I'd better go home." Not daring to look at Damon again, she left the table and pushed through the swinging doors leading to the kitchen.

The cook stood at the sink washing dishes. The maid was covering a bowl of leftover salad with plastic wrap.

"I'm not feeling well, and I need to leave," Deborah told the maid. "Could you get my jacket, please? It's blue wool with a red lapel pin."

"Of course. I'll bring it right away." The woman put down the bowl and hurried from the room.

The cook peered at Deborah through large, black-framed glasses. "I hope my cooking didn't make you sick." She rinsed a copper pan and set it in the drainer.

"No, your dinner was wonderful," Deborah assured the woman. "I might be coming down with the flu." She glanced over her shoulder, expecting to see Damon come through the doors, but no one appeared until the maid returned with her coat. "Is there a back door I can use?" Deborah slipped into her jacket. "I don't want to bother Jay and Lacey."

"You can go through there." Holding up a spoon dripping soapsuds, the cook gestured to a doorway leading to the back of the house.

"Thank you." Gripping her purse, Deborah hurried toward the door.

"Deborah!" a voice called.

Deborah's skin turned cold. Damon?

Jay came through the swinging door and crossed

the room. "Deborah, what's wrong? You look pale."

"Oh, Jay, I have to leave. I'm not feeling well." She rubbed her forehead.

Jay laid a hand on her shoulder. "Then you'd better stay here. You can stay all night."

She jerked up her head. "No! I mean, no, thanks. I need to get home. I'm sorry to run off without telling you, but I didn't want to interrupt your party. I planned to call tomorrow and explain."

Jay frowned and dug his fingers into her shoulder. "I really think you should stay here."

"No, I can't. Good-bye, Jay." She pulled away, and before he could stop her, she slipped through the back door. Outside, the cold air hit Deborah's face like a splash of ice water. She ran to the front of the house where her SUV was parked in the driveway. She kept looking over her shoulder, expecting to see Damon, or perhaps Albert, coming after her. But no one appeared.

When she reached her SUV, she jumped in, started the engine, and sped down the driveway. At the intersection with the main road, Deborah braked—and skidded. As predicted, the roads were icy.

The sound of another car engine back at the house sent her heart racing. A glance in the rearview mirror revealed bright headlights swerving onto the road behind her. Was someone deliberately following her? Or had another guest left the party, too?

Worry about the other car distracted her, and too late she realized she was on Ridge Drive, the route she and Milo took the night of the dinner party. She'd have to be extremely careful because the road had sharp curves and steep cliffs.

A car was still behind her, and she was sure it was

the same one that left the party right after she had. When she sped up, she noticed the other car increase its speed. She slowed, and the other car slowed, too. She passed several turnoffs, but the other car passed by them as well.

The cold truth finally sank in, and she gripped the wheel tighter.

She was being followed.

Deborah pressed the accelerator, but she dared not drive too fast. Her headlights showed a layer of ice glazing the entire road. Gradually, the other driver shortened the distance between them. The bright headlights prevented her from identifying the car's make or any other details.

Deborah's palms turned clammy, and her heartbeat knocked against her ribcage. Would this road never end? By now, she expected to be descending into Fairfield, but the curves and dips kept on and on. She passed the lookout where she and Milo had stopped to view the lights of Fairfield. How long ago that night seemed now.

Oh, Milo, where are you? If you were with me tonight, this wouldn't be happening.

A sharp curve lay ahead, with a steep ravine on her side of the road. A metal guardrail protected the shoulder at the ravine's steepest level, but the first part had no barrier.

As Deborah reached the curve, she glanced in the rearview mirror. The other car's bright lights nearly blinded her. Expecting the car to ram her bumper, she gripped the wheel, waiting for the impact. Instead, the car swerved around to her left side and, with the clank of metal on metal, slammed into her fender. The driver intended to run her off the road and over the cliff. Waves of terror washed over her.

The other car rammed her again. Deborah's SUV careened onto the shoulder. She would have to brake or hit the guardrail. If she hit her brakes, she would skid. Only a few seconds remained to decide.

She jerked her foot from the gas pedal and lightly pumped the brakes. But light pumping didn't work. Deborah's car spun in a complete circle and then headed straight toward the cliff.

She braked again but the car slid on the ice. Her pulse raced, and she squeezed her eyes shut, ready to plunge over the side. Instead, and to her utter astonishment, the SUV lurched to a halt. She opened her eyes to see nothing but blackness out the windshield. Holding her breath, she twisted and peered out the back window. The car must be somehow anchored to the guardrail, which kept the back wheels on the road's shoulder—and kept her from falling completely into the ravine.

The other car was nowhere in sight.

Deborah turned to face forward. Her heart hammered so fast she thought she would pass out. She forced herself to take a deep breath. Then another, and another. Maybe, just maybe, she could get out of this predicament alive. But she had to keep her head. She must not panic.

She found the door handle, but the door was caved in and would not open. Cautiously, she climbed over the console to the passenger's seat. The shift of her weight caused the car to slant a couple more feet toward the cliff. Deborah held her breath. She was close to freedom. But how much movement could the car take before it broke away from the guardrail and plunged into the ravine?

Inch by inch, she moved to the passenger's seat and gripped the handle just as headlights appeared, coming from the direction in which she had been traveling. Hope surged within her veins. Now she would be rescued. Sure enough, when the vehicle reached her SUV, it slowed. Deborah raised her arm and waved. But then the car sped again and passed by. Sick at heart, she slowly lowered her arm. Why didn't the driver stop to see if anyone needed help?

However, in the next few moments, the car made a U-turn and traveled back along the road, stopping with the headlights beaming on Deborah's car. Her spirits rose once again. She wasn't being abandoned, after all, and waved again. She even managed to open the door an inch or two. Her car creaked ominously, but the back end remained secured to the guardrail.

The driver's door of the other car opened. Someone stepped out and passed in front of the headlights.

A woman with swept-back hair and wearing a long coat.

Lacey.

Lacey? Deborah stared. What was she doing here? She couldn't be the one who'd forced her off the road. Deborah opened her car door a little wider. "Lacey! It's me, Deborah!"

Lacey stood there, gazing at Deborah. "Why'd you have to come back to Fairfield, Deborah? Why didn't you stay away forever?"

Deborah started to say, "Just get me out of here," but then Lacey shifted her position, and the headlights illuminated something she wore around her neck.

185

Something round and shiny. A pendant. A round and shiny gold pendant.

Chapter Eighteen

The memory that had only partially returned at the party now flooded Deborah so fast she gasped. Once again, she was running down the path at Rainbow Falls, on her way to Carla. Something shining in the woods caught her eye. She stopped to investigate. The object was this pendant on a chain of thick, gold links, then as well as now, worn by Lacey Grant. Lacey, looking wild and disheveled, and clutching Carla's green knapsack.

What was Lacey doing with Carla's bag? What was Lacey doing at the falls, period? The conclusion Deborah reached was too shocking to accept. No, Lacey couldn't have anything to do with Carla's fall. Not Deborah's best friend, Lacey Grant.

Deborah was torn between running to Lacey and continuing down to the rock where Carla lay. Of course, reaching Carla first was imperative. The young girl might still be alive. Oh, she hoped so.

Deborah turned to follow the path. But only a few steps later, she had tripped over an exposed root and hit her head on a rock.

Now, with her memory of those moments finally restored, relief washed over her. The feeling lasted only a second or two, though, because now she, not Carla, was Lacey's target. Tonight Lacey planned to kill Deborah. Deborah knew that as surely as she knew she was trapped in her car. Her teeth chattered, and panic

Linda Hope Lee

washed over her in wave after horrible wave.

Calm down! Use your head, and find a way out of this nightmare.

If she could keep Lacey talking, she might think of a way to escape. Or, hopefully, help would arrive before Lacey carried out her evil plan. Deborah stuck her head out the crack in the door. "Lacey, I know you were at Rainbow Falls the day Carla died."

Lacey strode to the edge of the cliff and stood with feet planted apart and arms folded. She was close enough to reach out and grab Deborah's hand—if she had wanted to.

"Finally got your memory back, did you? Too bad. Too late."

"Seeing your pendant just now brought all my lost memory back. But I haven't seen you wear the necklace since that day at the falls. And I didn't see it earlier tonight."

"You didn't see the pendant tonight? I thought you saw it when I unwrapped my anniversary gift, and that was why you ran away."

"The necklace was Jay's present? Then how could you have worn it at the falls?"

Narrowing her gaze, Lacey fingered the ornament's gold links. "I threw away the other one and told Jay I lost it. Then he found one just like it for our anniversary. But if you didn't see it tonight, why'd you leave?"

"I saw Damon's round tie clasp, and my memory trickled back. I thought he was the one I saw at the falls."

Lacey pressed her hand to her lips. "Then I didn't have to run you down."

"I would have remembered the truth eventually. You killed Carla, didn't you?"

Shoulders slumped, Lacey looked away. "I tried to talk her out of telling Jay's secret, but she wouldn't listen. I lost my temper. I shoved her, and she fell. I grabbed her knapsack to pull her back, but it came off and she kept falling. And falling…"

"Oh, Lacey…how horrible." Tears sprang to Deborah's eyes.

Lacey fisted her hands. "I couldn't let her ruin our lives. You know how hard I've worked for what Jay and I have."

"Did you kill Piper, too?" Deborah looked over Lacey's shoulder, hoping to see headlights, but the road remained dark.

"I had to." Lacey's mouth twisted. "She was close to finding out about Jay, too. I made her death appear accidental. Clever, don't you think?"

Deborah gasped. "Then you're the one who's been attacking me."

"I hoped you'd change your mind about living here, but you didn't. And when I learned you went to the doctor, I was terrified you would remember you saw me that day."

Her body went still, and Deborah took a deep breath. "You pushed me down the stairwell."

"Obviously not hard enough."

Hearing Lacey's cruel tone, Deborah winced. "And you stalked my house at night."

"My disguise worked, didn't it?" Lacey sighed. "If only you hadn't come back to Fairfield, we wouldn't be in this mess now."

Now she had Lacey's horrible confession, but she

was still trapped. After hearing all that Lacey had done to drive Deborah from Fairfield, Deborah had no doubt that tonight she'd try again. Would appealing to Lacey do any good? "Lacey—"

"Your car should have gone over the cliff just now. Since it didn't, I'll have to give it some help." She took a step toward Deborah's car.

"Lacey, please…"

"Shut up! No more talking. Someone might come by."

Lacey strode to the back of Deborah's car.

Deborah's pulse raced. Was Lacey strong enough to push the SUV away from the guardrail? The way the car bobbed around, sending it all the way over the cliff wouldn't take much. Through the back window, Deborah saw Lacey hunch down and disappear from sight. The car lurched forward, knocking Deborah against the dashboard. She had to get out. Now. *No matter what.*

She leaned into the open door and looked down. Blackness. She had no idea how far away the ground was. She didn't want to jump, but which would be worse, to jump, or to be in the car when it tumbled over the cliff? Deborah took a deep breath and jumped. Blackness sped before her eyes. Long, agonizing seconds passed before she crashed to the ground. Her left leg hit something hard, followed by the sickening crack of breaking bones. Pain spiraled up her leg.

Moments later, a scream filled the night air. Deborah looked up to see her car fly by, nose forward like a dive-bomber. Then she gasped at a horrible sight. Lacey was attached to the rear bumper, arms and legs flailing.

The car plowed into the ground and tumbled over, tossing Lacey about like a rag doll. The car rolled over again, finally crashing to a stop against the trunk of a pine tree.

"Lacey!"

No answer.

Again and again, Deborah called Lacey's name, but the only reply was the wind in the trees. Deborah staggered to her feet, but her injured leg buckled. The pain was so intense she feared she would lose consciousness. She must stay awake. Somehow, she had to get out of the ravine.

She peered up at the road. The headlights of Lacey's car beamed into the black night. Maybe someone passing by would stop to see what had happened. Shivers raked Deborah from head to toe. The cold had already penetrated her clothing. She would never survive the night.

Neither would Lacey.

If Lacey was still alive.

Deborah dragged herself to the embankment. By clawing at the earth, she climbed a few feet. Every inch gained took enormous energy. She had lost her shoes, and the cold ground quickly numbed her feet. Her injured leg throbbed, and her head spun. Still, she hadn't fallen more than fifty feet. With determination, she could reach the road.

Halfway up, unable to bear the pain any longer, she collapsed on the sloping ground. After a few minutes' rest, she would resume her efforts to reach the road.

In the distance, a car's engine hummed.

She raised her head to listen. Someone to help? Or more trouble?

The sound ceased. Her mind drifted. Then, a bright light swept into the ravine, and someone called, "Hello! Is anyone down there?"

She opened her mouth to call for help, but only a moan came out.

"Is anyone there?" the voice repeated.

The voice sounded familiar. Like Milo's. No, Milo was gone. Gone forever. Maybe the voice wasn't real but only part of a dream she'd drifted into.

The light shone on her. "I see you!" the person called. "Hang on! I'm coming!"

Someone skidded down the slope. Frost crackled and twigs snapped. The light wiggled and jerked, finally resting on her again.

"Deborah!"

"Milo?" Relief washed over her. "I-I can't believe you're really here."

"I am here, my darling." He knelt and cradled her head in his strong arms. His warm breath flowed over her cold cheeks.

"My leg…broken, I think. What are you…doing here? I thought…"

He placed his finger over her lips. "Shhh, explanations later. I've called for help…should be here soon. The experts will get you out of here. Until then, I'll keep you warm." Milo lay beside her and held her in his arms.

Wonderful warmth seeped through Deborah. "My car's down below," she whispered. "Lacey is, too. I called, but…no answer."

"I'll tell the medics when they come." Milo brushed back her hair from her face. "Now, save your energy."

Presently, the wail of sirens filled the air. Looking up, she saw red and yellow lights flashing and people pouring from the vehicles. Then she must have lost consciousness. Her next awareness was of being in the ambulance, sirens roaring once again, and speeding through the night.

****

At Fairfield Hospital, Deborah awoke to bright lights and hovering doctors. She glimpsed Milo before being rushed into surgery to have her broken leg set. He was there afterward, too, when she was brought to her room. She mustered a smile and mumbled a few words.

He patted her arm and said, "Get some rest now. I'll be back later." Milo made good his promise, and that afternoon, he returned.

He looked more handsome than ever in his jeans and a brown leather jacket.

He pulled a chair close to her bed and sat. "How're you doing?"

"Pretty good. The doctors thought I might have some internal injuries, but all the tests and examinations came out negative. The only injury I have is a broken leg." She nodded at the cast on her left leg.

"You were lucky."

Deborah couldn't wait any longer to ask the question uppermost in her mind. "How is Lacey?"

Milo's eyes clouded. "She didn't make it. Too many injuries the docs couldn't fix."

Deep sadness stole over Deborah, and she said a prayer for Lacey, and for Jay, and the boys, too. She laid a hand on Milo's arm. "Lacey confessed to me last night that she pushed Carla off the path at the falls that day, and that she murdered Piper, too, and made her death appear accidental. Did she tell anyone else before she died?"

"She did." He put his hand over hers and squeezed her fingers. "The police questioned her, and according to a source I have at the department, she told them the whole story. I think she knew she was dying and didn't want anything on her conscience. She knew about the article Carla wrote, after all, and guessed what she was up to."

"So, as we thought, she forged the note from Doug to Carla, asking Carla to meet him on the path below the falls. But why go to such great lengths when she could've met Carla somewhere in town? Or invited her to the Grants' home on some pretext?"

"I'm betting Lacey had murder on her mind all along, and Doug would be blamed."

Lacey a murderer? The realization made her sick to her stomach. "What would his motive be? He was Carla's boyfriend."

"I don't know." Milo frowned and shook his head. "Maybe she thought the police would believe they had an argument and he lost his temper and pushed her. He is a hot-headed guy."

Deborah shivered as she recalled her tense confrontation with Doug. "That's for sure. But why didn't Lacey kill me at the falls, too?"

"We'll never know for sure, but I'm guessing she didn't realize you saw her. You were running down the path, and she was hiding among the trees. When she saw you fall, she took the opportunity to escape."

Deborah nodded. "Then later, when I said I'd seen something shiny before I fell but couldn't remember what it was, she was afraid I'd seen her—or, rather, her pendant."

"Yes. And that's exactly what happened."

"Lacey was incredibly strong. I could hardly believe it when she pushed my car over the cliff."

"I'm sure her anger pumped up her strength, too."

Deborah shook her head. "Lacey always felt inferior because of her poor upbringing. She wanted Jay to be headmaster, so she could have the status and wealth she craved. But I don't think she was ever really happy."

"No, she wasn't," Milo agreed.

Deborah was silent a moment, and then another thought occurred. "When my car went over the cliff, Lacey appeared attached to the fender. But how could that be?"

"Apparently, when she bent over to push the car"—Milo made a shoving motion with his hands— "the chain of her pendant caught on a jagged piece of fender that broke when the car hit the guardrail. The pendant's chain was heavy enough to hold her to the fender as your car plunged into the ravine."

"So the pendant caused her death," Deborah mused. "How ironic." She cast him a cautious glance. "You haven't told me why you were driving along that road last night."

Milo took Deborah's hand in both of his. "I was on my way to the party, to be with you. I'd finally come to my senses and realized what a fool I was to let the most beautiful and wonderful woman I've ever known slip through my fingers because of something that happened in the past."

Tears sprang to Deborah's eyes. "Oh, Milo…"

"You were right—forgiveness has always been

hard. But I have forgiven you." He smiled. "I know you did the best you could the day of the accident. We don't live in a perfect world, even though I might wish we did. I have to accept that mistakes are made and accidents happen."

"I've forgiven myself, too." She brushed away a tear. "Beating up myself for that mistake accomplishes nothing. I want to get on with my life."

"I'm relieved to hear that. Carla's poor choices put her in danger. She didn't deserve what happened, but she certainly played a role in her fate."

Deborah's heart ached. "Does knowing she was a blackmailer hurt a lot?"

"You bet it does." Milo looked away and swallowed hard. "I wish I had known how mixed up she was. I'd have taken her to see Bob Lawton. But I didn't know. And I'm sure neither Mother nor Ed knew."

A lump formed in Deborah's throat. "I'm sorry for Carla."

"I know you are, my dear. But she will not come between us again." Milo caressed Deborah's cheek. "I love you, Deborah."

He loved her? For a moment, she was speechless. Finally, she found her voice. "Oh, Milo, I love you, too."

"Will you marry me?"

A declaration of love and a proposal of marriage? Surely, she was dreaming. But no, this was real. She saw the love in his eyes and the anticipation on his face as he waited for her answer. "Yes, I will marry you. Nothing would make me happier than to be your wife." Deborah spoke the truth. Spending the rest of her life with the man she loved with all her heart exceeded her wildest dreams.

Milo laughed. "That's exactly what I wanted to hear."

The kiss they shared held more love than Deborah had ever known.

Chapter Nineteen

Ten months later.

"We had a lovely wedding ceremony yesterday, didn't we?" Deborah posed the question to her new husband while sitting beside him as they drove along the road to Castletown.

Milo took his gaze off the road long enough to send her a warm smile. "We did."

They'd said their vows in a Fairfield chapel in front of a small group of friends. Now—after one very important stop—they were on their way to honeymoon at a mountain lodge.

With Milo's help, Deborah bought out Hank Dobson's half of the property and opened her bed-and-breakfast in January, as planned. Thanks to a successful summer season, the venture was profitable. She enjoyed her role as hostess, and although she'd now hired a live-in manager, she planned to remain active in the business.

"I'd better watch for the turn-off." She shifted to look out the window. Sure enough, around the next bend the sign popped up: "Rainbow Falls, Next Right."

Milo placed his hand over hers. "You're sure you're okay with this?"

She squeezed his fingers before letting go. "Yes, I am." She spoke the truth. Their visit to the falls today had a far different purpose than last year's trip.

A few minutes later, they pulled into the parking lot at the falls. After Milo helped Deborah from the car, he took a bouquet of chrysanthemums from the back seat. "Ready?"

She met his solemn gaze. "Yes, I'm ready."

They walked along the dirt path to the lookout. The bright autumn sunlight filtered through the trees, and a soft breeze stirred the leaves. The roar of the falls filled the air, blending with the twittering of the birds flying overhead. At the gazebo, they watched the falls tumble to the bottom of the canyon, while underneath them the floor vibrated with the water's power.

Holding tightly to Milo's hand, Deborah followed him down the narrow path to the bottom of the falls. Mist from the cascading water filled the air, sprinkling Deborah's skin and adding moisture to the breeze.

At last they reached the flat rock at the bottom. Milo handed her the flowers, and she knelt and laid them on the rock. "Rest in peace, Carla," she whispered.

Milo bowed his head. "Rest in peace, dear sister." They stood there a few minutes longer, and then he gently tugged her hand. "Time to go."

Before beginning the return trek, Deborah looked up at the top of the falls. She widened her eyes and gave a little gasp. "Look, Milo, a rainbow." She pointed to where the band of sparkling colors arced from the top of the falls and then disappeared in the trees.

Milo tilted his head to gaze upward. A grin spread across his lips. "And a beautiful one, at that."

"This is the first rainbow I've ever seen here, and how fitting we should see it today."

Milo put his arm around her and held her close. "I believe this is a sign our future will be very bright."

"I think so, too. Very bright, indeed."

Happiness and peace filled Deborah. She'd come a long way since that fateful day five years ago. The tragedy of Carla's death presented her with great challenges, but with Milo's help she conquered them. Now, she looked forward to a wonderful life in the years ahead.